It was impossible
little facet of his a

Dark hair, cut in a casual, tousled style, sat above a wide, intelligent brow. Striking eyes—shaded somewhere between grey and green—held a devilish twinkle. A sensuous mouth was tilted in a slightly lopsided smile, creating slashing dimples in his cheeks and making a frisson of heat skitter along her spine.

Then, like a flash, the name came to her and, forcing a small smile, she held out her hand.

"Dr. Herrera. What a pleasant surprise."

A large, warm hand engulfed hers, sending a shock of awareness up her arm, but she somehow held her smile in place and didn't pull away.

His eyebrows rose, and his smile widened. "I'm surprised you remember me. It's been a long time."

Oh, she remembered him all right. He'd been incredibly gorgeous, intelligent and personable…

Dear Reader,

I'll be honest and say that the older I get, the more fascinated I am by the knowledge that love can find you when you least expect it, and at any age. That sometimes it sneaks up on people, often seeming to offer up not just an unexpected partner, but also one who, on the surface, seems completely wrong for them.

In *Night Shifts with the Miami Doc*, I throw two people together who really, really don't want any more entanglements in their lives.

For my driven, professional heroine, Dr. Regina Montgomery, relationships have never been a priority and, as she's gotten older, seem to cause more problems than they're worth.

Dr. Mateo Herrera has shouldered more responsibility than most men his age, and now that he's free to pursue a life of his own, he has big plans for his future.

Neither is expecting that a chance reintroduction will lead them into the sort of conundrum they'll have difficulty extricating themselves from.

Inspired by the sultry heat of Miami and the Florida Keys, I'm hopeful you'll enjoy a minivacation with Latin music and warm days by the sea and will love these two as much as I do.

Ann McIntosh

NIGHT SHIFTS WITH THE MIAMI DOC

—

ANN McINTOSH

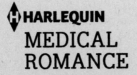

HARLEQUIN

MEDICAL
ROMANCE

HARLEQUIN®
MEDICAL
ROMANCE™

Recycling programs
for this product may
not exist in your area.

ISBN-13: 978-1-335-40435-0

Night Shifts with the Miami Doc

Harlequin Enterprises ULC
22 Adelaide St. West, 40th Floor
Toronto, Ontario M5H 4E3, Canada
www.Harlequin.com

Printed in U.S.A.

Ann McIntosh was born in the tropics, lived in the frozen North for a number of years and now resides in sunny Central Florida with her husband. She's a proud mama to three grown children, loves tea, crafting, animals (except reptiles!), bacon and the ocean. She believes in the power of romance to heal, inspire and provide hope in our complex world.

Books by Ann McIntosh

Harlequin Medical Romance

A Summer in São Paulo
Awakened by Her Brooding Brazilian

The Nurse's Pregnancy Miracle
The Surgeon's One Night to Forever
Surgeon Prince, Cinderella Bride
The Nurse's Christmas Temptation
Best Friend to Doctor Right
Christmas with Her Lost-and-Found Lover

Visit the Author Profile page at Harlequin.com.

For my beloved sister, Pia, and all South Florida medical and hospital support staff.

CHAPTER ONE

Sixty-eight-year-old Mrs. Morales not only looked unwell, she looked terrified, too. According to her chart, she'd collapsed at home, by all indications from an arrhythmia that caused her to faint. After being examined in the ER, she'd been admitted for further tests and monitoring, but although her heart seemed to be the main concern, Dr. Regina Montgomery had her doubts.

"Ask her how long she's been suffering from the swelling in her ankles," Regina requested of the assisting nurse, who, thankfully, spoke Spanish. "And the abnormal itchiness. And ask again if she's been experiencing muscle cramps."

As nurse Amelia Jackson relayed the questions, Regina took another look at the chart, displayed on her tablet. Some of the test results had come back, all focused on heart function, but, like the emergency room doctor before her, she was wondering if heart disease was Mrs. Morales's main problem. They'd asked for a cardiology consult, but it was Regina's responsibility as internist to ensure that if the patient needed additional treatment, it was provided.

"She says the swelling started about eight months ago, but she was itching before that. Only occasional muscle cramps, though," Amelia told Regina.

All classic signs of kidney problems.

"Has she seen a nephrologist?"

That earned her a skeptical look from the nurse, but she dutifully asked the question anyway, and was met with a breathless spate of words in reply.

At the frantic tone in the elderly lady's voice, Regina looked up to see tears streaming down her wrinkled cheeks. Putting down the tablet, she grabbed a couple of tissues from the handy box beside the bed.

"It's okay, don't be upset." Trying to soothe the older woman, she placed a hand on one shaking shoulder and held out the tissues. The last thing they needed was the patient's already elevated blood pressure going higher. She turned to the nurse. "What is she saying?"

"She's scared," Amelia replied. "She's only been in the US for a year, and it sounds as though her medical care has been spotty. I don't think she trusts doctors very much."

Mrs. Morales looked from Regina to Amelia and back again, and Regina was struck by the mute appeal in her eyes. It made her wish she could speak to the older woman directly, explain that she understood.

"I get it," she said quietly, using the tissues, which Mrs. Morales seemed not to have noticed, to mop gently at her patient's cheeks. "My grand-parents came to America when they were older, too, and they were the same way—only going to the doctor when the pain got too bad to bear. Tell her not to worry, that we'll take good care of her. Have you been able to contact her son?"

"Yes, but he's in Tampa, so it'll take a while for him to get back to Miami. He's a construc-tion worker, and the group had traveled there to-gether. He's getting on a bus as soon as he can. He also asked his wife to come to the hospital, but she has to arrange for someone to take over her shift before she can leave work."

While Amelia spoke to the patient, gesturing to Regina, Mrs. Morales reached out her hand. Regina hesitated only for an instant before tak-ing it gently and receiving a tremulous smile in return.

While looking at the chart, Regina hadn't put on gloves, and now noticed the texture of Mrs. Morales's skin. The older lady's hand was well-worn, her fingers and palm roughened by work and age. It brought to mind walking hand in hand with Granny through Brooklyn, and with it came the sense of safety and happiness she'd experienced at the time.

How she wished she could give those sensations back to her patient. But all Regina could do was smile and give the trembling fingers a light squeeze. It was tempting to stay where she was, giving comfort, but unfortunately it wasn't possible.

She had too much work to do, and acting as a locum was no excuse to be lackadaisical.

"Please tell her I'll be checking on her test results, and I'll be back in a little while to update her."

Then, with one last squeeze, she let go of the older woman's hand, and left the room to hurry the lab for the rest of the information she needed.

Once Mrs. Morales had been transferred up from Emergency, Regina, as internist on duty, was in charge of her care. It was up to her to ensure the older lady got the appropriate treatment and saw the right specialists. Similar as it was to her usual job of intensivist, there were enough differences to keep her happy, and as she walked toward the main desk, she couldn't help noticing one of the biggest ones.

Any speculative looks she received were because of her newness, not because of her personal life.

She couldn't afford any blemish to her character, because although things had improved, as a woman, and a minority one at that, she had to be that much better than her peers to make it to the top.

And making it to the top—to Chief of Medicine—was her goal.

One unexpected and distressing moment had lowered her reputation, and she'd struggled to continue to act normally afterward.

"Take a vacation," her friend Cher had said. "By the time you get back, the rumor mill at the hospital will have something else to talk about."

But vacations weren't part of her plan. She'd never taken them, unless she needed extra study time or wanted to attend a conference. As far as she was concerned, if it didn't bolster her résumé, it was a bit of a waste.

Then she'd found a site that matched doctors with hospitals in need of locums, and signed up. Accepting a seven-week stint in Miami served two important purposes: taking her far away from San Francisco and the uncomfortable situation she'd found herself in, and showcasing her versatility. She was out of the ICU, where she usually worked, and on the wards, handling a different set of patients and diseases. The variation, and the challenge it presented, appealed to her, too.

"A change is as good as a rest," her mother always said, and after two days in her temporary position, Regina was inclined to agree.

She really felt as though a weight had been lifted off her shoulders.

Getting to the desk, she gave the nurse behind it a slight smile—the kind that showed she appreciated how important all the nurses were but was calculated to keep a professional distance.

"Could you contact the lab and ask them to put a rush on the rest of Mrs. Morales's results, please? Especially the ACR and creatinine level tests."

"Of course, Doctor."

The nurse reached for the phone, and Regina looked down at her tablet, getting prepared to look in on her next patient.

"Please contact me when the results come in," she said, already walking away.

Once she had that information, she could decide whether she needed to bring in a nephrologist or not. Until then, rounds awaited.

Dr. Mateo Herrera shifted to tuck his phone between his chin and shoulder, so he could sign the form nurse Janie Curtis held out to him.

"I don't belong here, Mateo." The sound of tears in his sister's voice wrung his heart. "Everyone is so smart and so put-together, and I'm a mess."

"None of that is true, Serena. You're one of the smartest people I know, and all those people you think have everything together are only pretending, believe me." No eighteen- or nineteen-year-old had it all together, but some were more adept at pretending than others.

"Why'd you make me come all this way to college? I bet you were glad to get me out of the house."

She was working herself up to a full-on anxiety attack, but Mateo knew getting angry would only make it worse.

"Sure I was," he said easily, letting a hint of amusement tinge his voice. "Which was why I was trying so hard to encourage you to go to UM." The University of Miami was only forty minutes away from their house, and Serena could have lived at home if she wanted to. "If I remember correctly, it was someone else who wanted to go all the way to Gainesville."

He heard Serena inhale, and waited to see if his tactic had been effective or she'd go off on him. To his relief, she sighed.

"Yeah. You're right." He could usually count on her common sense to prevail in the end, and today was no different. "But I don't think I'm going to make it here on my own."

Instead of annoying him, her words filled him with deep warmth, since they showed how strong the bond between them was. Yet, he couldn't let his protective instincts win out over the knowledge that Serena needed to spread her wings.

"Okay, listen. You've only been there for a couple of weeks. Give it your best shot, and if you still hate it that much by the time you come home for my birthday, we'll talk about you transferring."

"All right." It was grudging, but at least she sounded as though she'd gotten her frazzled emotions under control. "Oh, hell! I have to be in class in twenty minutes. Gotta go."

"Love you," Mateo said quickly, knowing her habit of hanging up before he was ready. "Call me later, if you want."

"K."

Then she was gone.

Janie gave him a sympathetic look. "Your sister's first time living away from home?"

He smiled and nodded, unsurprised that she knew who it was he was talking to, since most of the people he worked with were aware of his family's story.

"She'll settle in quickly. My daughter cried on the phone to me every day for three weeks, and then suddenly I couldn't even get her to call me back, she was so busy and happy."

"I hope you're right," Mateo replied.

"You'll see," she said with conviction, then it

was back to business. "They've called for a consult on the fourth floor." She slid a slip of paper
toward him. "Should I get Dr. Timmins to go?"

Mateo glanced at his watch. He had an hour
and a half before the biweekly clinic for patients
with chronic kidney diseases started.

"No, I'll go." He picked up the paper and
headed for the elevators, but his thoughts were
still with Serena.

The child psychologist he'd consulted with
eleven years ago, after his parents' deaths, had
warned that of his three adopted siblings, Serena
would probably have the hardest time coping.
She'd been eight at the time, but unlike the other
two children who'd been a part of the family for
six and seven years, she'd only been adopted
by Emilio and Isabella Herrera the year before.
There hadn't been time for her to completely accept she was an integral part of the family, and
at that age, might even try to blame herself for
their deaths.

And the psychologist had been right. Serena
needed more reassurance than the other two put
together, but the effort had been worth it to see
her turn into the beautiful young lady she'd become. Now, if she could just build up the confidence to stay at the University of Florida, he'd
be happy.

As he stepped into the elevator, he pushed

thoughts of his family responsibilities aside. It was hard to do, since he'd been father figure, caregiver and everything else to his three younger siblings all these years. But they were, for the most part, all grown up now, and he knew he had to start stepping back and letting them live their own lives.

Not that he'd ever stop being there for them, in whatever way they needed. To abdicate that responsibility would be like thumbing his nose at his parents and their wish to give their adopted children a happy, loving family and a good life.

They hadn't lived long enough to see their dreams come true, but Mateo was dedicated to carrying the torch for them, no matter what he had to give up to do so.

On the fourth floor, he went toward the desk to check in, pausing as he heard a voice both strange and familiar.

"Has anyone come down from Nephrology yet?"

"Not yet, Dr. Montgomery."

Montgomery? Regina Montgomery?

Something stirred, hot and low, in Mateo's belly at the name and the memories it and her voice inspired. Drawn forward by excitement and surprise, he took the couple steps necessary to see around the intervening wall to where the woman in question stood.

Wow.

It may have been eleven years since he'd last seen her, but Regina Montgomery was as gorgeous and as sexy as he remembered. Back then, he'd been one of the residents under her supervision and, as such, had to maintain a respectful professional distance. It hadn't stopped him from experiencing hard-to-contain desire each time they'd interacted.

She was tall and statuesque, elegant in a cool, untouchable type of way. Her smiles back then were considered: just enough to show she was amused or engaged, but not enough to draw you in. She'd kept everyone at a firm yet polite distance. With eyes that unusual shade of dark gold, you'd expect them to spark with sunshine, but instead, they gleamed with the hauteur of a lioness.

Everything about her had made him want to ruffle her, get her messy, make her belly-laugh—anything to break that tranquil facade.

But that wasn't all he'd dreamt of doing.

Her smooth, dark bronze skin made his fingers itch to touch. The containment, so essential to her character, had him wild to crack it open and see what lay beneath. Something about her every move, thin smile or brisk order made him want her more.

At the time he'd thought it just a young man's fantasy—lusting after a woman ten years older than him had such a puerile ring to it—but now it seemed he hadn't outgrown the impulse.

In fact, with the way his body stirred and hardened, it seemed the attraction was as strong as it had ever been.

The surprise of seeing her here in Miami sent a seismic shock wave through his system, and he drew a deep breath, pulling himself together before he moved forward.

"Dr. Regina Montgomery." Although he tried to make the words friendly and professional, he heard the hint of roughness in his tone. "Fancy seeing you here."

CHAPTER TWO

HEARING HER NAME in an unfamiliar male voice made Regina stiffen and, for some strange reason, had the hair on her nape stirring. It was difficult not to spin around immediately, but she forced herself to pause and then turn slowly, eyebrows raised.

The sight of the man striding toward her made her breath catch in her throat, even as her brain scrambled to ignore his sheer beauty and come up with his name.

But it was impossible not to take note of every little facet of his appearance. Dark hair cut in a casual, tousled style sat above a wide, intelligent brow. Striking eyes—shaded somewhere between gray and green—held a devilish twinkle. A sensuous mouth was tilted in a slightly lopsided smile, creating slashing dimples in his cheeks and making a frisson of heat skitter along her spine.

Then, like a flash, the name came to her, and forcing a small smile, she held out her hand.

"Dr. Herrera. What a pleasant surprise."

A large, warm hand engulfed hers, sending a shock of awareness up her arm, but she somehow held her smile in place and didn't pull away.

His eyebrows rose, and his smile widened. "I'm surprised you remember me. It's been a long time."

Oh, she remembered him all right. He'd been incredibly gorgeous, intelligent and personable, so much so that women in the hospital had made thinly veiled innuendos about wanting to be on the *night shift* with him. There'd been no mistaking what they'd meant, and realistically, she'd felt as though a shift in his bed wouldn't have been a bad idea. But there was no way she'd risk her reputation and goals by suggesting such a thing, or even intimating it.

Even if he'd expressed an interest, and she'd been willing to indulge, as his supervisor it would have been extremely inappropriate.

But of course, she didn't say any of that.

"I like to think I remember most of the residents I supervise," she lied mildly, loosening her fingers so he let them go. "I take it you're the nephrologist I've been waiting for?"

It seemed very important to move the conversation away from anything even remotely personal, and back to work.

"I am," he replied, that smile still on his face

sending another skitter along her spine. "What do we have going on?"

She handed him the tablet, Mrs. Morales's chart already on the screen, and left him to look it over as she spoke to the nurse about another patient. It was, after all, her standard way of dealing with specialists—she provided them with the information they needed, and left them to draw their own conclusions.

Her need to focus anywhere but on Mateo Herrera had nothing to do with his looks, or the warmth swirling just beneath her skin.

Besides, he was probably married, with an equally gorgeous wife—who'd happily given up her own ambitions to become his appendage—popping out beautiful babies at respectable intervals. Somehow that image was enough to tamp down the rush of interest she felt at having those incredible eyes and lovely grin aimed her way.

Interest she had no business feeling, since she was totally and completely off men.

"You're right to be concerned." Regina looked up in time to see Mateo slide a calculator into the pocket of his lab coat as he spoke. "Let's go and look in on Mrs. Morales. I'm going to need to do a full workup on her."

She held up her hand to stop him from walking away.

"Before we go, you need to know that Mrs.

Morales doesn't speak much, if any, English. Spanish only."

There went that lopsided smile again. Regina tightened her lips to stop herself from smiling back, but silly heat gathered in her chest, threatening to rise into her face.

"I'm fluent," he replied, waving her ahead of him down the corridor. "There's sometimes a bit of confusion with idioms and localized dialects, but between me and the patient, we can usually work it out."

"Great," she replied, heading off, chastising herself, despite knowing her reactions were normal. No red-blooded woman could avoid being affected by this man. She was sure of it.

"That's one of the things I remember best about you—your refusal to make assumptions about anything, even whether a man named Mateo Herrera can speak Spanish or not."

Keeping her gaze firmly trained ahead to avoid looking at him, she replied, "In our line of work assumptions can kill. I'm always checking myself to make sure I'm not taking shortcuts or allowing implicit bias to throw me off track."

"I think I remember hearing you tell one of the residents that exact thing." She could hear the smile in his voice but steadfastly refused to check and see if it was reflected in his eyes. "So, when did you move to Florida?"

The change of subject surprised her, and she replied without thinking. "I haven't. I'm here as a locum for six weeks, filling in for Dr. Nguyen while she's on maternity leave."

"Hmm… Does that mean you've left Charthouse Memorial and become an itinerant doctor?"

He sounded skeptical, and Regina shot him a frowning glance but saw only curiosity in his expression.

"Would that be a bad thing?" She heard the defensiveness in her voice and cursed herself for it. What she chose to do with her life was none of his—or anyone else's—business.

"Not at all. In fact, it sounds interesting and almost idyllic. I just pictured you rising to the top somewhere, and I doubt you'd be able to do that, moving from place to place."

He'd surprised her again, because his assessment of her ambition was spot-on. Somehow hearing that made her relax her usual rigid rules regarding discussing personal matters with colleagues.

"I left Charthouse about six years ago, but I'm still in the Bay Area." Charthouse was the teaching hospital where Mateo had started his residency. She'd been offered a more lucrative position across the Bay, in Oakland, and with the opportunity for advancement, she'd taken it.

"I recently decided I needed a change, but not a permanent one, so I took sabbatical leave, and here I am."

"Staving off burnout?"

There was no mistaking his curiosity now, but she'd be hung, drawn and quartered before she discussed with him her reasons for taking time off.

"Something like that," she replied, making her voice brisk and rather quelling.

"I see." They'd reached the door to Mrs. Morales's room, and Mateo took hold of the handle but didn't open it. "Well, I'd like to invite you out to dinner, as a welcome."

Oh, hell no. She hadn't come to Florida to get tangled up in any kind of relationship, even a friendly one. And if she was reading the gleam in Mateo Herrera's eyes correctly, he definitely had a different type of entanglement in mind.

So a crisp but polite "No" was what she intended to say. What came out of her mouth instead was, "With you and your wife?"

His eyebrows rose.

"I'm afraid I don't have one of those. Never got around to it."

A playboy, then. Or a liar, since she couldn't fathom why such a prime specimen of man was still on the shelf.

It would be stupid, though, to lie to her about

it, since they were working in the same hospital and it wouldn't take much to check through the grapevine.

Before she could come up with a fitting response, Mateo continued, "What about you? Did you end up marrying that neurosurgeon you were dating?"

That he would remember something so trivial surprised her—and caused her unwanted but unmistakable delight.

"How on earth did you remember that?"

He shrugged, his lips quirking. "I think it was the bunches of red roses he kept filling your office with that made it stick in my mind."

A huff of amusement broke from her lips before she could stop it. "Ah, that was in the waning days of our relationship, when he was trying to convince me that marrying him, and giving up my career to have his babies, was the best thing that could happen to me."

Mateo's eyebrows almost disappeared into his hairline this time. "Did he ask if that was what you wanted?"

"Why would a neurosurgeon want to know what was going on in his girlfriend's brain?" she deadpanned, and was rewarded with Mateo's laughter.

Yet, he was still blocking the door, and it seemed that the sensual gleam in his eyes deepened.

"So you're not married?" he asked, and although neither of them had moved, he seemed closer, and the conversation far too intimate. An electric current ran between them as his eyes darkened, and it took every ounce of control not to lick her lips and to keep her face impassive.

"Never got around to it," she replied, using his own words, but giving them a clipped, almost dismissive edge.

That seemed to get through to him, since he only nodded and opened the door, standing back so she could pass.

As she did, her entire side warmed, as though from his body heat, although she knew full well it was just her heightened physical awareness. There was something about Mateo Herrera that made her decision to avoid men seem far harder than it should.

Oh, she's one cool customer.

Regina sailed past him like a queen, leaving a clean, slightly flowery scent eddying in her wake. Mateo inhaled deeply, savoring it, along with the knowledge that despite her demeanor, the attraction he felt wasn't one-sided.

He wasn't sure how he could be so certain, but he was. Trying to figure out the clues that led him to that conclusion would be an interesting exercise for later, but right now he had a patient to see.

The seduction of Regina Montgomery would have to be delayed—but he was determined it wouldn't be denied. Fate had gifted him with an opportunity he wasn't prepared to pass up.

Since the last of his siblings had moved out of the house they'd all shared, he'd been overtaken by an ebb in energy and a sense of drifting without purpose. Spending time planning out a new, more focused future hadn't stemmed the sense of lassitude hounding him.

Now he suddenly felt rejuvenated. Reinvigorated.

And it was because of the woman who'd preceded him into the room.

She seemed to embody the type of no-strings-attached adventure he needed to get him out of his present funk.

There were four beds and three patients, with Mrs. Morales in the farthest one from the door, on the right. Unlike the other two women, she was awake, and watched as Mateo pulled the curtain around her bed closed.

Then she held out her hand, and Regina took it, as though it were the most natural thing in the world.

That, too, was something he remembered from when she'd been his supervisor—her innate ability to put patients at ease, without seeming to work at it at all. She was neither jocular nor overtly friendly, but something about her calm competence spoke loudly to patients and their families alike. Seeing how she interacted with patients and how they responded to her had stuck with him and given him an ideal to aspire to. While their personalities were very different, he now realized he'd unwittingly adapted his bedside manner to achieve the same result.

Greeting the patient and introducing himself in Spanish earned him a tentative smile, but he saw Regina use her free hand to pat the old woman's, as though to comfort her.

He kept his voice soothing, and coaxed the information he needed from Mrs. Morales in small chunks, hoping to keep her calm. From the chart he knew her blood pressure and heart arrhythmia were problems, and didn't want to exacerbate them by being too pushy.

Besides, she kind of reminded him of his paternal grandmother, so she brought out the gentle side of him.

By the time he'd finished examining Mrs. Morales and gotten her history and symptoms, the elderly lady was smiling and calling him *Papito*. She even reached up and patted his cheek. Glancing at a silent Regina, he saw her fighting back a smile. Or maybe laughter.

He could hardly stop himself from grinning back.

"I've explained to her that, with her symptoms, we need to do further testing on her kidney function, and she's agreed," he said to Regina. "Until I have those results, it's impossible to know whether diminished kidney function is causing her heart problems, although it's a definite possibility."

"That was my concern, too," Regina said, giving Mrs. Morales's hand one more pat before releasing it. "I'm still waiting for Cardiology to send their recommendations, but I'd like a complete picture before I proceed."

The door from the corridor opened as Mateo was making notes, outlining the specific tests he wanted run, and he looked up when one side of the curtain was thrown open, revealing cardiologist Dr. Morgan Welk. Behind him was one of the younger cardiologists, whose expression suggested he'd rather be anywhere else but where he found himself.

Or perhaps it was the company he was being forced to keep that gave him that rather uncomfortable look. It wasn't be any surprise to Mateo, who found Welk to be an irritating bully.

It took every scintilla of professionalism Mateo had to keep his expression neutral and not allow his dislike of the older man to show.

"What are you doing here?" Welk asked, his tone aggressive. "This is a cardiac patient."

Before Mateo could reply, Regina spoke, her voice calm but with an unmistakable thread of steel running through it.

"I called for a nephrology consult on Mrs. Morales."

Welk slowly turned his gaze her way, lifting his chin, looking down his nose at her, despite the fact that he was actually shorter.

"And you are?"

"Dr. Montgomery, internist in charge of Mrs. Morales's care."

"I don't know you." Now he sounded peevish, as though having someone new in the hospital was a personal affront.

"Nor I you," she replied. She even had that cool, distancing smile still firmly affixed on her face, as though neither annoyed nor surprised by the older man's behavior. "Yet, here we are."

Welk's mouth opened and closed a couple of times, as though he could hardly believe what he was hearing.

"Now, young lady—"

"Dr. Montgomery," Regina interjected, her smile not wavering for an instant. "And you are?"

Once more Welk seemed stunned, but then, with something that sounded suspiciously like a curse under his breath, he spun on his heel and headed for the door.

"I won't have my time wasted like this," he said, over his shoulder. "When you get your act together, let them know upstairs."

"Thank you," Regina replied, making sure he could hear her clearly. "I'll make a note on the file that Cardiology refused to examine the patient or give their input."

That stopped him in his tracks, as it would any doctor in their right mind. Just thinking about what the legal department would have to say should something like that come to light was enough to make even an ass like Welk rethink.

When Welk turned back around, his face was red, and he spoke through clenched teeth.

"That isn't the case. But I don't have time to waste, trying to work around Herrera, while he does…whatever it is he's doing."

"Not a problem," Mateo said, taking a leaf out of Regina's book and giving the older man a thin smile. "I'm finished."

Then he took his leave of Mrs. Morales, telling her he'd see her in a little while, and stepped away from the bed.

"Let me know your thoughts, please, after you reexamine Mrs. Morales." Regina spoke to Welk in the same calm way, but again the hint of steel was clear. "I've been waiting for the cardiology report."

Then, before he could do more than growl, she gave Mrs. Morales a smile and a wave, and was on her way out of the room.

Mateo was only a step behind her when she got to the door, and he held it open for her to go through.

If he'd been attracted to her before, it was

nothing in comparison to how he felt now, having seen her so effortlessly and efficiently put Welk in his place. He wanted to see her away from the hospital, finally get a chance to break through that cool shell, to see what lay beneath.

Yet, having seen her handle Welk, he knew he'd have to step lightly, even when everything inside wanted to push, to insist. Even to demand.

But before he could say anything, Regina beat him to it.

"About dinner... I don't think it would be a good idea."

A casual approach seemed the best bet, although he was feeling decidedly eager to get her to himself, even if just for a while. So he gave her a bland smile.

"What's so bad about two old colleagues who haven't seen each other in years having a bite to eat and catching up?"

Her gaze searched his, and her lips tightened just a little at the corners.

Then she shrugged. "When you put it like that..."

Yes!

CHAPTER THREE

By the evening after her first seven-day shift, Regina felt as though she had a handle on the way the hospital worked. Pouring herself a glass of wine, she stepped out onto the tiny balcony of her executive rental and subsided into a chair.

Taking a deep breath of the warm night air, she let it out again on a sigh. Back in San Francisco, the temperature would be in the fifties—if they were lucky—but here in Miami it was warmer, and dry. She'd laughed to herself, hearing some of her new workmates complain about the January cold. Apparently, anything under eighty-five degrees was an excuse to pull on a sweater, or even a coat.

She was fine with a light cardigan, and was even barefooted, as was her habit at home.

Stretching her tired neck muscles, she tried to relax and let go of the stress that had built up during the week. Although the schedule was lighter here than back in California—seven days on call, then seven off, rather than two weeks on and two off—getting used to a new routine was taxing. As was getting called out three of the seven nights, when a patient needed her urgent attention.

Even building a working rapport with the staff she interacted with the most took its toll, but she felt as though she'd achieved that.

Well, except with Morgan Welk, who seemed bent on trying to undermine her whenever he could. It didn't bother her, since she'd learned, from a very young age, how to deal with people like him. When faced with that kind of opposition, she became more determined, and made sure to ruthlessly cross her *t*'s and dot her *i*'s, so as to never be found lacking.

The only real fly in the ointment, as far as she was concerned, was the upcoming dinner with Mateo Herrera, which was scheduled for the next evening.

Every time she thought about it, an internal battle ensued.

Her sense of self-preservation told her not to go.

But her adventurous side, which she hardly ever let out to play, wanted to see where this all would lead.

Oh, he'd tried to make it sound merely casual and friendly, but Regina hadn't been fooled. The truth was in his eyes, which gleamed darkly whenever he looked at her, and seemed to make all kinds of naughty promises.

Promises she was both eager to take him up on, and a little afraid of, too.

Or maybe she was just overthinking? After all, he was at least ten years her junior. Why on earth would he be interested in an older woman, when he could have his pick of all the younger ones?

So she should go, and they would have a nice dinner, and that would be that.

And if it went any other way, she'd just shut it all down.

That was also something she was very good at—setting boundaries and steadfastly disallowing anyone to cross them.

But each time she'd had to interact with him, she found herself feeling slightly off-kilter.

And excited.

It had taken her all of three days to actually admit that to herself, but her physical reactions whenever he was around couldn't be ignored. Yet, hadn't she decided to cut men, with their ridiculous demands and deceit, out of her life?

That decision had been firm and definitive, brought about by the kind of situation no self-respecting woman ever wanted to be caught in. And even four months later she couldn't shake the shame and anger of being accosted by a strange female in the hospital parking lot and accused of being a home-wrecker.

Regina had been speechless. She really hadn't known Kevin was married. In the ten months they'd been seeing each other, it hadn't even crossed her mind to doubt he was as single as he'd claimed to be. They'd slowly been getting closer to the point where she'd have considered a commitment, which he professed to want from her, but she'd been in no rush. First, she was studying for her master's degree in hospital management, then she'd been putting in a lot of hours to position herself for the next promotion she wanted.

Only afterward, in hindsight, had she realized how easy she'd made it for him to perpetrate his deception.

With her work schedule and complete focus on the upward trajectory of her career, she'd been a prime target. He canceled on her? No problem. She'd just moved on to the next thing on her to-do list, which was always long, and meticulously written down. With her sights set on the long term, she was too busy to worry about a few missed dates.

He'd completely fooled her, and her takeaway from the experience was—no more relationships. No more messy interactions that would detract from her plans or open her up to ridicule. Being the cynosure of all eyes at work because she'd made a stupid mistake had become too much, even for someone who normally paid no attention to what others thought.

Which was why it annoyed her to no end to find Mateo this attractive.

To feel her insides melt and heat and quicken whenever he was around, as she wondered what kind of lover he'd be.

Thank goodness for a well-developed poker face and the ability to keep her feelings to herself. Those attributes had served her well, although occasionally she'd caught him looking at her in a way that suggested he was seeing right through her facade. And what he'd gleaned was as exciting to him as he was to her.

After agreeing to go to dinner with him, Regina had given him her address and phone number, and expected him to call or text sometime over the next few days. Most of the men she'd dated had gone for the hard sell: calling all the time, laying a foundation to get her to sleep with them, treating her like a challenge or competition.

Instead, there'd been radio silence, leaving her to stew about whether Mateo was at all interested in her.

She couldn't remember feeling this way about any other man.

If she were made of less stern stuff, Regina mused to herself as she sipped her wine, she'd be terrified.

There was no way to know which way her dinner with Mateo would go. He'd been completely professional whenever they interacted in the hospital, which was almost daily, as they'd worked together on diagnosing and treating four patients, including Mrs. Morales.

It was a good thing they'd come up with a diagnosis and treatment plan for the elderly lady before her daughter-in-law had arrived. The younger Mrs. Morales was a firecracker, and had made it clear she was there to take charge of her mother-in-law's care going forward.

Regina was glad to see the obvious affection between the two women, and the gentle way the younger woman treated the older. And when Mateo came into the room, her patient waved toward him and called him *Papito*, which made her daughter-in-law laugh.

When Regina had asked Mateo what it meant, he'd looked a little sheepish, and the tips of his ears got adorably red.

"It's just a silly nickname," he'd said, trying to sound dismissive.

"But what does it *mean*?" She wasn't sure why she couldn't let it go, when it was clearly not something he wanted to discuss.

"Um, strictly translated, *Little Daddy.*"

She'd bitten the inside of her cheek so as not to laugh at the grudging admission.

When she'd fought for and won back her composure, she'd asked, "Do you get those kinds of nicknames often?"

It had been on the tip of her tongue to actually call him that, but she'd restrained herself at the last minute. It felt too intimate to tease him that way, and the last thing she needed was to get even friendlier with him.

"Occasionally. Now, about her treatment schedule…"

Letting him off the hook was harder than she liked. And she'd subsequently had to stop herself from calling him *Papito* a couple of times thereafter.

There was something about him that brought out her lighter side, and, coupled with her physical attraction toward him, it made him all the more dangerous.

Sighing again, she took another sip of wine and then lifted her face up to let the night air flow across her overly warm skin. Just thinking about him made her hot and jumpy, and she searched for some justification that didn't involve wanting—quite desperately—to sleep with him.

It was, she decided, just a side effect of all she'd been through, and being in a strange place.

A place that seemed to hum with electricity unlike any she was used to. Redolent with a sort of carefree, beach vibe on one hand, and the frenetic energy of a racing, hustling city on the other.

Mateo Herrera was just one more facet of a brief change that had, understandably, given her usually work-focused, driven life a shake-up.

But in the final analysis, nothing that happened here in Miami was going to have a lasting impact on the life she'd mapped out. She wasn't planning on sleeping with Mateo, or on possibly opening herself up to the same kind of gossip and ugliness she'd fled San Francisco to get away from.

If she just reminded herself of that and kept her eye on her long-term goals, it would all work out fine.

Lifting her glass, she silently toasted her own determination, before tipping the last of the wine into her mouth.

Nothing—and definitely no *man*—was going to stand in the way of her achieving her goals.

Not even one as delectable as Mateo.

Mateo pulled into the parking lot of Regina's building on the night of their dinner and drove under the portico. She'd told him she'd meet him in the lobby, but traffic had been lighter than he expected and he was fifteen minutes early.

He wished he'd timed it better, since sitting in the car, waiting, gave him far too much time to think. His nerves were jangling, his pent-up excitement tightening his muscles and making his mouth dry.

It was a while since he'd been on a date, but that wasn't the problem.

What made it nerve-racking was that it was a date with Regina, a woman who made him ravenous each time he looked at her, and brought out in him a fierce, almost feral, desire.

Whenever he saw or thought about her, his brain seemed to freeze, to stumble over itself, even as his body reacted in far more carnal ways.

Waiting for her to appear had anticipation tingling through his body, and made him feel like a teenager again.

It wasn't a comfortable sensation in the slightest.

He couldn't recall feeling like this on past dates. Not that he'd had time to do much dating while raising his siblings.

At first, he'd thought that once they grew up and things settled down, he'd have time to go back to his old life. Of course, he was wrong. As a nominal single parent, things had just gotten more complicated. There was a constant round of school and extracurricular events he had to attend, as well as making sure he was keeping them on track scholastically and emotionally. Even as they became teenagers and wanted to do their own thing, he realized he couldn't release the reins just yet. In fact, to him, that had been the most critical time.

Those early teen years were when so many young lives went off the tracks, and it was his responsibility to make sure they all stayed on the straight and narrow, and were happy.

Now he was free—or as free as he'd ever be—and it seemed he was sorely out of practice when it came to women. The few casual relationships he'd been able to slip in without disrupting his home life apparently hadn't prepared him for this.

But he was probably just being silly, he told himself, as he glanced at his watch. While he was certain of his electric attraction to her, he wasn't 100 percent sure it was reciprocated. And he knew, for a fact, that if Regina Montgomery decided there would be nothing between them, he couldn't change her mind.

She was too determined a woman, and he was too much of a gentleman. Strong-arm tactics weren't in his nature, and he had no intention of adding them to whatever small dating repertoire he still possessed.

They'd probably have dinner, chat about inconsequential things, and that would be that. Not that he wouldn't make his interest known, but no matter how badly he wanted her, he'd make sure to leave the decision on what happened completely up to her.

He'd been watching the lobby, and each time the elevator doors opened his heart skipped a beat. Just as he glanced at his watch again, he saw movement out of the corner of his eye and looked up.

This time his heart not only stuttered but seemed to turn right over, leaving him breathless.

She was absolutely stunning.

Her electric blue long-sleeved top wrapped across her shoulders and under her breasts, hugging every curve and making her waist look tiny. The tantalizing hint of cleavage had him wanting to kiss all the way along it and down, so as to discover the mysteries lying below. A silky skirt in vibrant colors flowed around her legs and clung enticingly to her thighs as she walked. High, strappy sandals completed the sexy ensemble, and her hips swung with each long stride.

It wasn't just her looks that kept him entranced. The way she carried herself—so proudly, regally—made the need inside burn hotter. He was totally enraptured, frozen where he sat, his heart pounding, blood racing through his veins like lava.

Then she paused, looking out through the glass, reaching up to touch her hair, as though to make sure the long waves were still in place. She normally wore her hair up, and Mateo's fingers itched to tunnel through it, rub her scalp until she purred.

He bit back a groan, annoyed at his reaction. *This is ridiculous.*

Tearing his gaze away, he reached for the handle of the car door and made himself open it. Wasn't it just a few moments ago he was calling himself a gentleman? Time to get his head on straight and start acting like one, rather than a sex-starved teenager.

As he got out of the car, she saw him, and although her face didn't light up the way he'd have liked, a little smile tipped her lips. And it was a more relaxed, natural one, than the thin, distancing smile she usually gave.

He got to the door to the apartment building just before she did, and when she pressed the lever to unlock it, he held it open for her.

"Hi," she said, sailing past him and leaving a sweet waft of perfume behind. It went straight to his head, like scotch. "I hope you weren't waiting too long."

"Not at all. And I have to say, you look very nice."

Of course, she looked way more than just nice,

but he knew better than to be too effusive. He'd seen the way she coolly cut down any comment that even hinted at flattery or kissing up.

His comment still earned him a slanted, sideways glance over her shoulder, as he reached out to open the passenger door.

"Thank you," she replied, rather wryly, as she slid gracefully into the seat. "I wasn't sure where we were going, so I hope I'm dressed appropriately."

He bent to tuck the end of her skirt properly into the car so it wouldn't get caught in the door, bringing their faces almost level. This close, her beauty stole his breath, but it was her gleaming, lioness eyes that caught and held him.

Was it his imagination, or was there more than just amusement in those molten depths?

"No matter where we go, you're dressed appropriately," he replied.

"So it's the hotdog stand, then?"

Now there was no mistaking her teasing, irrespective of her dry tone. It was there in her gaze and the upward curve of her gorgeous, sensual lips.

He chuckled, wanting to kiss the smile off her mouth, but forcing himself to straighten instead.

"How did you know that's my favorite spot in Miami?" he asked. "I made a reservation for the bench closest to the cart."

"Lovely," came her swift reply. "As long as they serve the dogs with sauerkraut, I'm happy."

"What?" He feigned outrage. "Not on your life. This is chili country, lady."

Light laughter greeted his statement just before he shut her door, and he was still chuckling as he rounded the hood of the car. The silly levity made the evening feel less fraught, although the laughter did nothing to quell his desire for Regina.

If anything, her quirky sense of humor intensified it, even though nothing in her demeanor led him to think she was interested in him physically.

Either way, he thought, as he opened his own door, the evening should be fun.

And he was content with that.

CHAPTER FOUR

REGINA SETTLED BACK against the soft leather seat and smiled ruefully to herself.

Although she'd dithered back and forth a bit while trying to decide what to wear, in the end she'd dressed for seduction—wearing a blouse that showcased her boobs, and a skirt that tended to outline her legs as she walked. Everything she had on, down to her silky, lacy lingerie, was carefully chosen to scream *Sex!*

Just when she'd decided a little fun and games with the delectable doctor would be okay, she wasn't sure. All she knew was that at some point the realization had struck—this might be the last time she had a chance to totally let loose without fear of the consequences. And she figured she might as well let him know straight up.

And what was Mateo's reaction?

You look very nice.

She had to bite the inside of her cheek not to laugh out loud.

So much for going for the obvious.

Almost even more annoying was how incredible he looked, and her reaction to seeing him get out of the car.

Used to him being in scrubs, which he made look ridiculously yummy, she found that seeing him dressed for the evening gave her an even better appreciation of his good looks and fine body. His white linen shirt made his shoulders and chest seem even wider than usual, and his dark dress pants showed off powerful thighs.

Her heart had trip-hammered, and a surge of heat rushed through her, settling deep in her belly. It wasn't like her to have such a visceral response to a man, and it had taken her aback. Then she'd reminded herself that she'd spent the last week thinking about him and wondering whether there might be something about to happen between them.

Well, since he'd just said she looked *nice*, she could relax and put that thought aside. If he were interested, she was sure he'd be more explicit with his compliments.

Most of the men she'd come into contact with were.

Yet, his nonchalance made her tension dissipate, and she decided to simply enjoy the evening. At least it seemed they shared a similar, ridiculous sense of humor, so that would make things easier, although why she felt comfortable sharing that with him was debatable. Only her closest friends were privy to that side of her.

Not wanting to go down that road mentally, she asked, "So where is this hotdog stand we're going to anyway?"

They'd stopped at a red light, and he turned to give her a grin.

"Over on Miami Beach. It has a really nice outdoor seating area with a view of the beach, and hopefully it won't be too cool to sit out there. Sometimes they have a live band, too."

He went on to explain that the restaurant was owned by a famous Miami power couple who'd translated their musical success into a number of lucrative businesses.

"Sometimes she even comes out and sings with the band."

"That would be cool," she said as they got on the highway. "I love her voice."

Just before he could answer, his phone rang, and since it was paired with his car, the name *Serena* flashed on the screen set into the dashboard.

Hmm... Who's that?

"Excuse me," Mateo murmured, before connecting the call. "Hey. What's up?"

"Are you at home?"

The voice sounded young, and the question seemed loaded, so Regina couldn't help watching Mateo out of the corner of her eye, waiting to see how he reacted.

There was no change at all in his demeanor as he responded, "No, I'm not."

"Darn it." Serena's disgruntlement was clear. "I can't find my white, fleece-lined hoodie, and wanted you to look to see if I left it there."

Curiouser and curiouser.

What was the relationship between Mateo and this Serena? Clearly a close one, and the wave of anger and, strangely, betrayal that washed through her made the breath hitch in her suddenly tight chest.

"I know that's not the only warm hoodie you have. We bought a bunch before you left."

"But that's my favorite."

"Unless you've undergone a radical change in habits since leaving home, I suggest you dig through the pile of laundry in your room. It's probably there."

The sound that came though the speaker was clearly a huff, and Regina saw Mateo's eyebrows contract. Then his lips twitched in an abbreviated smile.

"Am I wrong about the pile of clothes?" he asked, letting his amusement bleed over into voice.

After a little silence, Serena sighed. "No."

"Okay, go look there. And if you still can't

find it tomorrow, let me know and I'll look in your room."

Another sigh. "Okay."

"Good girl," he said, his gentle tone somehow going straight to Regina's heart. "Talk to you tomorrow. Love yah."

"Wait. Where are you anyway? What are you doing?"

"None of your business," Mateo replied, putting on his indicator, signaling his intention to exit the highway. "Bye."

He disconnected the call just as they were going down the ramp, and Regina could see the still-tender smile on his lips.

"Sisters," he said, ruefully. "Terminally nosy."

Ah, that explained it. Some of it anyway.

"I wouldn't know," she admitted. "I don't have any."

Mateo shot her a glance. "Brothers?"

"Nope. I'm an only child, and now glad of it."

He chuckled, then changed the subject, asking her how her first week at the hospital had gone, leaving her with a bunch of questions she wasn't sure how, or whether, to ask.

Why was his sister calling him about her jacket, rather than their mother?

How old was his sister anyway? Sounded like there was a big age difference.

And did this mean that Mateo—a grown man in his midthirties, at least—still lived at home?

Okay, there were several cultures that expected, even encouraged, their young people to stay in the family home, some even after they married. Was that the case with him, and if so, how did he stand it?

At eighteen Regina had fled her parents' home and never looked back. There was no way she'd have been able to continue living under her father's thumb, being told she'd never amount to anything more than a vessel to carry some man's children. She'd refused to be broken by his outdated and insulting behavior up until the end of high school, but it had gotten harder and harder not to start believing him.

No. The only way to make something out of her life had been to hightail it out of there and succeed in her chosen profession—thereby overcoming her early upbringing.

Even after her father died, it never occurred to Regina to go back home and live with her mom, or have her mother come to San Francisco. She doubted that even crossed her mother's mind, either, since they weren't particularly close.

Clearly, Mateo must have been far luckier in the parent department. But although she tried not to judge, she couldn't help mentally shaking her head. His living at home just seemed so incongruous.

Seemingly, behind that masculine exterior lay a mama's boy!

Yet, even as she had the thought, she knew she didn't actually believe it. No matter his living arrangements, Mateo was definitely his own man.

"How are you finding the schedule? Is it what you're used to?"

His question pulled her out of her contemplations, and she replied, "It's easier, in a way. I'm used to two weeks on call, and two off, and dealing with ICU patients tends to lead to more callouts or nights spent at the hospital. This week I only had to go in a few times for emergencies."

"So what do you plan to do with your time off while you're here?"

"I have some developmental courses I need to get done before the end of the year, so I'll probably buckle down to those."

He shook his head, those sensual lips coming together in an amused little twist.

"The end of the year, and you're thinking about them now, in January? How about sightseeing, or having some fun somewhere new?"

"It's not a vacation," she said, hearing the defensiveness in her tone. "My time is better served focusing on my professional advancement."

"You say vacation like it's a dirty word."

His amusement had her looking away, out the window. They were driving over a causeway, lights glinting on the water of Biscayne Bay. Somehow the beauty of it brought a sense of melancholy.

"I don't take a lot of them." Unwilling to elaborate, she left it there.

"All the more reason to make good use of the time here," he said easily. "There's so much to do and see within a couple of hours of Miami, it would be a shame to come all this way and not experience some of what's on offer."

Regina shrugged. "I'll see if there's anything that piques my interest."

From her peripheral vision, she saw him slant her a look, but he didn't pursue the conversation any further, instead starting to point out various interesting landmarks as they arrived in the trendy Miami Beach community.

At the restaurant, they were ushered through the sleek, stylish bar and indoor area, and onto the patio. Here, casual elegance was the byword, and the piped music was low enough that the sound of waves crashing on the shore could be heard above it.

"That cold front that came through a few days ago is still affecting the sea," Mateo said as he held out her chair for her. "Listen to those waves."

Regina couldn't help laughing lightly. "Those couple of days when it passed through, you'd have thought it was snowing, the way some of my colleagues were behaving. One came in dressed in a wool coat, scarf and knit cap."

He chuckled with her, laughter lighting his face and making his eyes sparkle.

"We Floridians take our warm weather very seriously, and make a huge stink if it's disrupted. I swear that's one of the reasons my sister has been fussing about wanting to come home. She's at college in Gainesville, and the temperature there was at least ten degrees lower than here."

He'd opened the door to that particular conversation, and Regina couldn't help wanting to walk through.

So after they'd ordered drinks, she asked, "How old is your sister?"

"Serena? She's nineteen. It's her first year at college, and she's having a hard time settling in. She has some social anxiety and self-esteem issues, so I'm trying, as best I can, to help her work through them and be able to stay where she is, rather than transfer back here."

Difficult to know the right questions to ask, so instead, Regina said, "It sounds like you're a very involved brother."

He looked up from perusing the menu, and his

brows came together slightly, just for a moment, and then he gave a wry smile.

"I guess you don't know my family story, but I've been guardian for my three youngest siblings for over a decade. They were the reason I gave up my residency in San Francisco and moved back here, after my parents died in a plane crash."

Her heart clenched in sympathy. Despite the time that had passed, she could still hear the sorrow in his voice.

"No," she said softly. "I didn't know. I'm sorry about your parents."

"Thank you, but it's okay. Well, long enough ago that I've gotten used to them being gone, although I definitely miss them every day, especially when one of the youngsters has a problem and I have to figure out the best way to deal with it."

Still trying to figure out the age gap, she asked, "How many children did your parents have?"

"Six. Three biological and, later, when we older ones were teenagers and getting ready to go to college, they adopted Ben, Micah and then Serena." His smile was tender and a little wistful as he continued, "Mom always said that we, as a family, had a lot to offer, but I think they adopted because she just really loved mothering. Lola, Cristóbal and I were all becoming independent, and didn't need that as much anymore, and she missed it."

"So when your parents passed away, you stepped in."

She wasn't surprised by the story, really. It was something she could definitely see him doing.

"It made sense. Lola had just gotten her dream job with a publisher in New York, and Cristóbal was working as a geologist with an oil company, so he was away more than he was home. I could relocate and rearrange my life without too much fuss."

Relocate and rearrange.

The words stood out to her and left her wondering just how much he'd given up to take up the mantle of guardian for his young siblings.

Did he have to rethink his specialty, knowing some were more labor-intensive than others?

What kind of social life had he been able to enjoy, with three kids to look after?

How had he managed, suddenly being thrust into the role of father figure?

Yet, those weren't things she was comfortable asking, so she kept all the questions she had bubbling inside to herself.

Instead, she simply said, "That must have been incredibly difficult for you—dealing with your grief and having to adjust to being de facto parent, too."

He looked back down at his menu, his expression calm, but he also shrugged one shoulder, as though in dismissal.

"It was what needed to be done, and what my parents would have wanted—no, expected—me to do. I have no regrets." Then he glanced up at her and smiled, saying, "So do you see anything that catches your fancy?"

She turned her attention to the menu, but she found herself staring blankly at it, consumed by a rare, tender emotion she had no name for.

This Mateo was a departure from the man she'd thought she was going out with, and she wasn't sure how to handle that revelation.

Instead of the drool-worthy hunk she was considering seducing, now she saw the quietly strong, truly admirable person. A man of stature, who'd shouldered responsibilities others would have run away from.

And as to that question he'd asked, about whether she saw anything she fancied…if she answered honestly, it would be to say, *Yes, you*.

Pulling herself together, she finally got down to picking something to eat, but a swirl of conflicting emotions kept battering her insides, and she wasn't sure what to make of them.

Part of her wished she could just ignore it all and enjoy a lovely dinner in this romantic spot without giving their conversation, and her feelings about it, another thought. But she knew herself well enough to admit that wasn't possible, and the damage had been done.

Mateo Herrera had not only gone up more than a few notches in her estimation but had also increased her attraction to him apace.

CHAPTER FIVE

MATEO LEANED BACK in his chair, replete from the delicious meal. Relaxed in a way he couldn't recall being for a long time.

It felt good to have adult conversation on a Friday night without worrying about getting home. Getting used to this new way of living was taking some time, but having Regina's company made it seem effortless, and well worthwhile.

The sense of loss he'd experienced when Serena left home had taken him by surprise. His older siblings had expressed their opinion that at least now Mateo could have a life of his own, one not predicated on the other kids' needs, and at first he'd agreed. But then reality had set in.

Almost everything, including his work schedule, had revolved around his siblings. With the immediate responsibility gone, he'd been adrift—perhaps even a little depressed.

But he was too young to have empty-nest syndrome, wasn't he? And it wasn't as though Ben,

Micah and Serena didn't still need him. Hell, he got calls from one or the other, or all three, almost daily. Although they were all young adults now, he was aware of being the linchpin of the family—the one everyone knew they could count on to be there, no matter what.

Sometimes he thought perhaps he was being egotistical, but the others had said much the same at various times over the last few years.

That they were glad he'd held on to the house their parents had lived in, so they could always come back home.

Or how grateful they felt to have him to talk to, or ask advice of.

Several times a year they all got together for birthdays, Thanksgiving and Christmas, always at the house in Miami, and it was during those times that Mateo felt the warmth of his parents' love most keenly.

His mother and father may be gone, but the family they'd built had survived, and that was the most important thing.

But an evening like this, spent with a beautiful and intelligent woman, made him all too aware of what he'd been missing while holding it all together.

They'd talked about all kinds of interesting topics, and, with some judiciously placed questions, he'd learned quite a bit about her. One of those things was just how ambitious she was, and her complete focus on her job.

"You did a degree in business, and then a master's in hospital management?" he'd asked, in total disbelief. "When did you have the time?"

"Well, I made the time," she'd replied, giving him a small smile. "But remember, I didn't have three kids to take care of, or much of a social life, either."

"Was the sacrifice worth it?"

She'd looked down at her plate for a moment, as though either dismissing or considering his words. Mateo realized which it was, when she met his gaze again.

"It will be, when I become the first black female Director of Medicine at the hospital."

There wasn't a hint of hesitation in what she said, or any doubt that it would, indeed, happen.

The urge had been there to question her confidence, but there was no way to do it without being rude. And it wasn't as though he didn't believe she could do it; he absolutely knew that she could. But there were hurdles ahead of her that he knew were out of her hands, and he couldn't help wondering if she had taken them into consideration.

Then she'd said the most telling thing of all.

"When I set my mind to something, nothing stands in my way. And opposition only makes me more determined."

She'd glanced down again, as though considering whether to say more, and he knew he had to respond. He wanted to understand her better, learn what made her tick.

"It's a good way to be," he admitted. "Not many people have that ability, and they crumble under pressure."

Her nod was curt, and her lips tightened fractionally.

"When they do, they give up their dreams, rather than fighting for them."

"Sounds as if you're speaking from experience."

Those lioness eyes suddenly seemed fiercer than usual, but then they softened with a flash of what he interpreted as sadness.

"My father didn't believe women should be educated, or that his wife should work. My mother wanted to be a lawyer, and she already had been accepted to law school when they met, but he dissuaded her from going back once they'd agreed to marry." She shook her head. "I decided at a very young age not to follow in her footsteps, and when he tried to browbeat me into looking for a husband right after high school, I left home."

Her words stunned him and made his chest ache.

"How did you manage?"

She shrugged, but he could see the tension in the stiff set of her shoulders.

"My grandmother took me in, and I worked my ass off to go to college, and then to medical school. I refused to doubt I could do it, even though my father said it was impossible."

Then she smiled and visibly relaxed.

"And after my father passed away, my mother went to law school after all. She was almost sixty when she graduated, but now she's an advocate for disadvantaged kids in Brooklyn."

"That's amazing," he said. "You must be really proud of her."

"I am."

It had been a sobering discussion. One that made him even more aware of how lucky he'd been in life. His father had amassed a fair amount of money in oil exploration, and his parents had always been totally and completely supportive of their children's ambitions.

It would have never occurred to either of them not to be encouraging and uplifting.

And the insight into another facet of Regina's personality added a new layer to the thrum of awareness he constantly felt being in her company, giving it a new depth.

Now, as she paused in the act of eating her dessert and watched the band setting up on the low, beachside platform, he gazed at her clear-cut profile, trying to discern what it was that attracted him so.

Yes, she was beautiful, and carried herself with almost regal poise, but that in itself didn't explain his overwhelming interest. Her razor-sharp intellect certainly contributed, yet also was just a part of the equation.

Then she turned to him and said, in that cool, contained way she had, "It's a shame they're just setting up to play when we're about to leave."

It struck him then, as it had in the past.

He had an overwhelming desire to ruffle her, break through the barriers she placed between them, and see the real woman behind the wall.

Oh, she'd probably say that what he saw was who she was, but now he knew, for a fact, that there were parts of her securely hidden away, and he wanted to see them on full display.

There had been a flash of that other persona in the way she'd taken Mrs. Morales's hand, as though it were second nature.

And another glimpse when she'd spoken about her parents, and the latent pain had so briefly been revealed.

Even the way she'd just spoken, distancing herself from whatever wish she may have to stay and hear the music.

At work she was forthright and fearless, but outside of it there was a subtle subtext of denying her own desires and emotions, as though to indulge them in any way would be a weakness.

"We could have a coffee," he said, catching the waiter's eye. "And at least hear a couple songs."

For an instant he thought she was going to refuse, but as the waiter approached, she said, "I think I'd like that."

As the waiter walked away again to get their drinks, Regina glanced to the left, over his shoulder, and her eyes widened.

"Is that...?"

He followed her gaze, in time to see the owner of the bar greeting a few people near the door leading to inside the restaurant. The famous singer smiled, exchanging a few words with the customers at each table as she passed.

"It is, indeed," he replied to Regina, unable to hold back his smile when he saw her amazed expression. Even she wasn't immune to being starstruck. "And it looks as though she's making the rounds. You might even get to meet her."

"You wait until I tell my friend Cher about this," she said, regaining her poise, but smiling wider than he'd seen her do before. "We used to belt out her songs in the basement when we were young."

It took a few minutes for the singer to get to their table, and when she did, her gaze tracked from Regina to Mateo, and back again.

"Good evening," she said, in her distinctive, slightly husky voice. "I hope you're having a good time here with us?"

"It's been wonderful." You'd never know from Regina's cool smile and calm voice that she'd just been geeking out over the other woman's presence. "Thank you."

"Will you be singing with the band tonight?" Mateo asked, hoping the answer would be in the affirmative. Hearing some of the songs she used to sing with her friend would make the evening all the more special for Regina, and knowing that made him bold enough to pose the question.

The singer gave him a bright smile.

"I've been thinking about it," she said. "If I do, will you promise to get up and dance?"

"Of course, if my lady agrees," he replied, and gained himself a little wink.

They both looked at Regina, who, after a brief hesitation, shrugged and smiled slightly.

"Why not?"

"Then I will," the Diva said, casting a knowing eye over their table, just as the waiter returned with their coffee. "By the time you've finished those, I should be ready."

When she'd moved on to the next table, Regina lifted her coffee cup but paused with it a few inches from her lips. "Do you even know how to dance to eighties music?"

"Nope," he replied, mirroring her actions and taking a sip of his coffee. "But I'll do my best not to embarrass you."

Her eyebrows rose slightly, and she shook her head. "I won't be the one embarrassed," she replied, with her customary insouciance.

And as Mateo chuckled in agreement, he also thought he was beginning to understand how to deal with Regina Montgomery's wall of reticence.

No pushing, no forcefulness. Make it her decision, always, and see where things led.

Not the easiest of paths for a man used to getting his own way a lot of the time, but one he would stick to, in the hopes of getting what he really wanted.

Regina Montgomery, naked in his bed, crying out with pleasure.

Regina sipped her coffee in silence, her gaze firmly fixed on Mateo's face. Torn between amusement and surprise, she didn't know whether to laugh or frown.

So she did neither.

Instead she tried to figure out his mindset from his expression.

She'd never countenanced being bossed around, and had quite a bit of experience with men who tried to do just that. Most of the time, men tried to push her to do what *they* wanted when she was reluctant. And the approach was either an aggravating macho shove, or a smug *I know what's best for you.*

Nothing got her back up quite like feeling as though she was considered an onlooker in her own life, unable to make the decisions that were best for her. At times like that she beat a hasty retreat, or administered a verbal smackdown guaranteed to let the other person know she wasn't up for it. At all.

Yet, she also wasn't used to being deferred to in quite this way. At no point tonight had she felt him exerting his masculinity, or acting as though to prove who wore the pants. Yet, he was no wimp, either, and their conversations had been spirited and lively, with both of them sticking to their guns when appropriate.

It was an ingrained impulse, this need to question his character and motivations. Unfair, perhaps, but necessary. She knew she wasn't imagining the attraction swirling between them, but past experience told her to be guarded, and watch out for the inevitable domineering traits to surface.

So she'd watch and wait, and enjoy herself in the meantime. The singer they'd just met was best known for a series of fast-paced pop hits of the eighties and nineties, and Regina had no objection to an energetic turn on the dance floor.

It would also be a great way to see Mateo in motion, too.

As she sipped her coffee, she looked forward, if she were honest, with a fair amount of anticipation to see what would come next.

The evening had been enjoyable, even though she'd found herself opening up to Mateo in ways she normally wouldn't. Speaking about her parents was something she rarely did, except with her oldest and closest friends. Yet, talking to him was so easy she'd hardly hesitated. He had a way of looking at her that made her feel see and heard, in the best possible way.

Perhaps even a little bit understood, although that, too, might just be an act.

The band started up, playing an instrumental rendition of a current hit, the upbeat song seemingly setting the stage for their boss's turn at the microphone. As the song was ending, Regina saw the Diva making her way up on stage, and the crowd all clapped and cheered.

Mateo smiled, and when the noise calmed down slightly, he leaned closer and asked, "Are you ready?"

Regina didn't think she was: not for the dance, and not for him, but she nodded anyway and took his hand when he held it out. As he led her away from the table, she was aware of some eyes turning their way, but most people were focused on the woman at the mic, and Regina paid no attention to the others. They didn't concern her.

But what *did* concern her was the fact that when the band started playing again, it wasn't one of the singer's dance hits, but one of her sultry, sexy ballads.

And the way Mateo looked down at her as they stopped at the edge of the dance floor, snagging her gaze and refusing to let it go, the gleam in his eyes making her heart beat an erratic tattoo.

She expected him to pull her close, but instead he simply squeezed her hand, and Regina found it was she who moved toward him and into his waiting arms.

Again he disconcerted her, by keeping a bit of distance between them as he placed his hand on the small of her back and began to move to the music.

Oh, the man could dance!

No rent-a-tile, as her granny used to call it, when she'd see people locked together on the dance floor, hardly moving. Instead he was master of the smooth, luscious sway and step, his only guidance to her coming from the light movement of his hand on her back, and the gentle motions of the other hand, holding hers.

As they swept across the floor, their bodies

brushed occasionally, lighting sparks to flash and sizzle beneath her skin. Regina realized she'd melted into the dance, was letting him set the pace and increase the elaborateness of the steps, and following him with complete trust.

Ceding to his calm, gentle, yet completely masterful control.

How crazy to feel secure and aroused by it all, at the same time.

To feel desire building, just as the singer's voice built with each repetition of the chorus.

To have heat—which had nothing to do with exertion—grow throughout her body, until she was all but aflame.

No longer able to hold his gaze, she let hers fall away, realizing her mistake when it dropped to his mouth.

Those lips, always sensual, were now firm, yet even sexier than before.

They seemed the embodiment of the same control he was now exerting over her body, as he led her through the most erotic dance she'd ever had.

And how she stopped herself from leaning just those couple of inches necessary and kissing him senseless, she would never know.

CHAPTER SIX

AS THEY WALKED back to the table, energy still thrummed through Regina, and arousal coursed, thick and hot across her skin. A glance at Mateo seemed to find him amused, unmoved by what had been for her one of the most—if not the most—sensual events of her life.

Mateo pulled out her chair and Regina sank into it, glad to be off her somewhat shaky legs. The Diva started singing one of her Latin-inspired dance hits, and Regina shook her head.

"That's not what I was expecting, when she asked if we'd dance," she said as Mateo helped her push her chair in toward the table. "I think we were set up."

He'd bent closer to hear her over the music, and his breath—warm against her ear—made her have to fight a shiver, when he replied.

"I think we acquitted ourselves well."

"Well, you certainly know how to move."

"It's in the genes. My mother was a dancer,"

he explained, before straightening and gesturing to the waiter for the bill.

She'd have liked to get more information about that, but the music was too loud, so she waited until after he'd paid and they'd stepped outside the restaurant to wait for his car.

"Did you say your mom was a dancer?"

Mateo smiled one of those tender tilts of his lips that came out whenever he spoke about his family.

"Yes. When she and my father met, she was dancing with a troupe in Buenos Aires, as a way to put herself through university. Once she got her degree, she stopped dancing professionally, but she still knew how to move. She taught all of us kids. Us older ones anyway. She didn't have the opportunity to teach the others."

The regret in his voice wrung her heart. He was clearly so devoted to his family and the legacy his parents left behind that she couldn't help but be touched.

Yet, it distanced her from him, too. Each story about his family seemed to highlight the differences between them. His childhood sounded like the dreams she'd had as a young girl, of a family filled with laughter and loving support—a fantasy to the woman who'd had to scratch and claw and sacrifice to make something of herself. In her mind, there was no point of intersection between them besides both being doctors, and the incredible lust she had for him.

Lust she wasn't even completely sure was reciprocated.

"So did you teach them?" she asked, continuing the conversation.

Mateo laughed, the sound both amused and rueful.

"You were definitely an only child," he replied, still chuckling. "I realized early on that while they'd accept me as an authority figure, none of my youngest siblings had any interest in learning anything like that from me. I offered, but both Ben and Micah looked horrified and declined, and—having learned my lesson—I enrolled Serena in dance class, figuring if she liked it, she could continue going."

Another dream Regina had had as a little girl that never came to fruition, but she pushed the slightly sour thought aside, to ask, "Did she like them?"

The valet pulled up in Mateo's car, and Mateo opened her door for her as he replied succinctly, "Two left feet, in that respect. She's a handy soccer player, though."

Regina found herself laughing as she watched him walk around the front of the car.

As he closed the door and reached for the

seat belt, he asked, "Nightcap, before I take you home?"

She hesitated, unsure of how wise it would be to spend more time in his company. Mateo created a rare maelstrom of emotions in her—desire, tenderness and, yes, even longing—that she instinctively knew was dangerous. But Miami was just a waypoint on the path to her ultimate destination. What harm could truly come from enjoying him while she could?

"Sure," she said.

Then, as he put the car in gear, she wondered if the nightcap he offered would be at his house. If it were any other man, she'd think so, but Mateo wasn't like any other man she'd been out with, and constantly surprised her.

And she still couldn't decide whether that was just his usual personality, or she was being played in some way.

Either way, she was determined not to lose her focus because of a pretty face and a winning persona. Not that she was usually susceptible to doing any such thing, but she couldn't be too careful.

The last few months had been stressful, and alleviating that stress by coming to Miami had also left her on slightly shaky ground emotionally. It was the first time in years she'd done something that wasn't directly tied to her long-term goal.

Sure, it would be an interesting addition to her résumé, but it hadn't been in the plan, and she chafed at the thought that this side trip might actually be detrimental to her career. Not that it was in the same category as the initial embarrassment over Kevin's betrayal, but there was always the fear that she'd diminished her worth at the hospital in San Francisco.

All those worries had, she realized, made her question every decision she made, almost obsessively. Even at work, where she was usually at her most confident, she found herself double- and triple-checking actions that were basic or routine.

"So what do you plan to do for the rest of the weekend?" he asked, pulling out of the parking lot and turning the car north.

"Actually, I have a distant cousin who lives in Boca Raton, and I promised to go visit her," she replied.

She'd been dreading going, just because she really didn't know Marilyn very well, and didn't know what to expect when she got there. Now, though, she was glad to have something to do, even if just so Mateo wouldn't feel as though he needed to step in and entertain her.

"I didn't know you had relatives here in Florida."

"This is my grandmother's cousin's family,

so, like fourth cousins twice removed or something like that?"

He chuckled. "I've never been able to work out those family connections. Everything is just 'cousin' to me."

They had left most of the nightlife behind and were crossing the barrier island, away from the sea and toward Biscayne Bay.

"Do you have a lot of family here?" She remembered he'd said his parents had met in Argentina, and was curious.

"I have an aunt and some cousins in Texas, but most of the rest of the family is in Argentina. When Mom and Dad died, my aunt Leona came from Texas and lived with us for about eight years. She'd gone through a divorce the year before, and I think she was happy to get away for a while."

"Did she bring her kids with her?"

Mateo put on his indicator and waited for a car to pass before making a left-hand turn into a dimly lit driveway. On either side were chain-link fences overgrown with flowering vines.

"They were all grown up by then," he replied. "She was older than my father by six years, and married fairly young."

At the end of the driveway was an electronic gate, which opened as the car approached. They drove through into a parking lot with a long, low, brightly illuminated building on the other side. Beyond it, there were glimpses of masts, and the occasional gleam of lights on water.

"Where are we?"

"It's a private marina and yacht club," he replied, slotting the car into a parking space. "It's a nice place to have a drink and see the city from across the bay."

"You have a boat here?"

The more she heard, the farther the distance between their life experiences seemed to grow. Private yacht clubs were still, even at her comfortable stage of life, beyond her reach.

"Actually, the membership belonged to my father, and he'd bought Ben a small sailboat one birthday, after he'd expressed an interest. The boat is still moored here, until Ben is settled and can decide what he wants to do with it, so he only gets to sail it when he comes home for holidays." He gave her a grin, as they both undid their seat belts. "I laugh to myself when I see Ben's dinky little boat up on a rack and compare it to the monster vessels tied up in the water, but, hey, it's still a boat, right?"

"That's true," she agreed, unable to stop herself from smiling with him.

There was just something about his wry amusement that sucked her in every time.

She opened the car door and got out. While

his earlier courtesy of opening for her was nice, she didn't want him to think he had to do it every time.

He met her at the front of the vehicle and offered her his arm.

Inside, the restaurant was to the right, and had just one table of patrons, while the bar, which ran the length of the left wall, was occupied by four older men, all huddled together at one end. The bartender smiled when he saw them.

"Dr. Herrera. Good to see you."

"You, too, Keith. How've you been?"

Obviously Mateo spent quite a bit of time here, Regina surmised, as the two men chatted casually for a minute.

"What will you have tonight, ma'am?" Keith addressed Regina, hands poised over the bar, as though just waiting to conjure a drink from thin air.

"A glass of chardonnay, please."

What she'd really have liked was a whiskey on the rocks, but she'd been careful to limit her liquor consumption.

Mateo was enough of an intoxicant as it was.

After Mateo opted for a craft beer, he took her elbow to lead her out through open French doors, across a flagstone-paved patio, and down two stairs to a concrete walkway that curved above the marina itself. The area was beautifully landscaped, and the view across Biscayne Bay was gorgeous.

Regina leaned against the balustrade and took it all in.

The lights of Miami gleaming on the water, and the fabulous yachts rocking gently in the foreground gave the scene an almost dreamlike ambience. And she was supremely aware of Mateo beside her, too, the heat of his arm resting on the concrete near hers, the smell of his cologne, his movement as he lifted the bottle to his lips.

She had to stop herself turning to watch him drink.

"How lovely," she said, trying not to fall too far under the spell of moonlight and Mateo, keeping her voice level.

"It's one of my favorite vistas," he replied, his low tone seeming to vibrate between them, causing goose bumps to shiver along her spine. "Whenever I want to think, or just catch my breath, I come here."

"I can see why," she said.

But she was aware of his having turned his back to the view. Now he leaned against the balustrade, and from the corner of her eye she could see him looking at her.

"I was thinking," he said, which was a conversational gambit that rarely boded well. "I have a villa down in the Keys. Why don't you come down with me one weekend? I have clinics on Tuesdays and Thursdays, but I can take Friday and Monday off and make it a four-day weekend. That will fit in with your schedule, right?"

"It would…"

Now she realized what it was about Mateo that confused her and made her hesitate to give him an answer.

Usually by now, she would have a pretty good idea of where things stood on a date—whether the man in question was interested in her, particularly if he wanted her physically. Mateo had been fun, interesting and a perfect gentleman. Once or twice she thought she'd caught a glint of something hot and fierce in his eyes, but it had never lingered long enough for her to be sure.

It made it impossible to know exactly what he was asking her when he offered to take her to the Keys, and because he hadn't made his intentions clear, she wasn't ready with a reply.

She was always ready with a reply, wasn't she? Always on the ball, knowing ahead of time what to say, how and when to say it. Instead, she floundered a little, feeling silly.

Then she pulled herself together. This waffling wasn't her style, at all.

Facing him fully, she said, "It sounds like fun,

but I haven't decided whether to sleep with you or not, so I can't judge whether it's a good idea."

His eyebrows rose, and for an instant, his eyes flashed. Then a slight smile tipped the edges of his lips.

"I don't see what the problem is. If you don't decide to be intimate with me, we'll still have a fun weekend."

Taken aback, she instinctively asked, "And if I do decide to?"

His smile widened and his eyelids drooped, giving him a feral, dangerous air.

"Then," he said, his voice low and intense, "we'll have an even better time."

Was it her imagination, or had he moved fractionally closer? Even if he hadn't, her reaction was the same as it would have been if he'd fully invaded her space. Her heartbeat kicked into high gear, and her skin suddenly felt too tight—hot and tingly.

The urge to turn away, to hide, was so strong it was all she could do to hold his gaze, which had once more turned bland, without even a hint of amusement.

"By the way," he asked. "How will you decide?"

"I have no idea," she admitted, taking a sip of her wine and turning back to the view. Trying for insouciance, although she felt anything but indifferent. "I'm sure I'll think of something."

Mateo threw back his head and laughed, the sound of his unfettered amusement taking her already wicked desire for him even higher.

She wished he would just take a hold of her, kiss her senseless the way she wanted him to, but she had already worked it out: he wasn't going to push or demand. Unlike her prior experiences with men, this man was determined to, on at least this level, force her to make the decision on her own.

No coercion.

No coy hints or attempts to get her to agree.

It was, for her, a novel situation.

Not that she was a pushover, just going along if a man crooked his finger. Far from it. If she wasn't interested, she had no problem saying so. But, looking back, she'd also never been the pursuer or the instigator—she was always too busy with her life and plans to expend the energy.

Or maybe just not as interested as she'd thought she'd been at the time. Every intimate relationship she'd had seemed easy at the time. The man chased; Regina decided whether or not she wished to be caught.

Now she was faced with a man who wasn't planning to make it easy for her, and something about that lit a fire in her belly.

Which was both arousing and scary at the same time.

"Well, let me know when you decide, both about the trip and about me," he said, the laughter in his tone still apparent. "Your next weekend off would be good, but I need to let them know by Monday if I'm taking those days off."

"I'll let you know by then," she replied, keeping her voice firm. Businesslike. But she already knew what she was about to do when she put down her glass on the ledge and turned to him. He was watching her, and she didn't allow herself to hesitate. She stepped close, as she had when they danced, but then closer still.

And kissed him.

Not just a peck, or a light brush of her lips. Regina, having decided on a course of action, never went with half measures. Nope. She went in hot, letting her intentions be known.

But although she instigated it, cupping his face and taking the kiss straight to erotic, Mateo didn't hesitate, either. In a blink he took over, one hand tunneling into the hair at her nape to angle her mouth into the perfect position. The other hand settled, hot and firm, on the small of her back, pulling her flush against his body.

She'd thought of it as an exploratory foray, a way to discover whether her interest in him was worth pursuing. In the past it had always been easy to separate her brain from whatever physical pleasure her body was experiencing. It was, she thought, a part of her nature—detachment was her stock-in-trade, and it had served her well over the years.

Being able to maintain critical thinking at all times was of paramount importance. It was what made her good at protecting herself from distractions, and great at her job.

Yet, in Mateo's arms, with his lips on hers, detachment deserted her before she even realized it was happening.

Sensation after sensation fired through her system, until she was a quaking column of need. His body, hard and hot, against hers. His lips, firm and masterful, not coaxing but demanding response. The sound of their breath, rushing, rushing from lungs laboring to take in enough.

Her head was swimming, and a moan rose in her throat.

That was when she pulled back, and was both relieved and bereft when Mateo let her go immediately.

Forcing herself to turn away, to modulate her breathing, to act as though the ground hadn't rocked beneath her feet, Regina reached for her wineglass. Only as she was lifting it did she realize her hand was shaking.

One more thing to try to get under control.

Putting the glass to her lips, she sipped, but not even the crisp tartness could erase the taste of Mateo from her consciousness.

She scrambled for something to say that would break the unbearable tension tightening her muscles and turning her legs to jelly. A witty remark. An off-the-cuff joke. But her brain was too busy reliving the kiss to spare her the time.

But there was no way she'd reveal to him just how shaken up she was from their brief, explosive embrace. So, gathering every ounce of the containment she was known for, she gave him a cool smile.

"I'll let you know about the trip to the Keys," she said, inordinately proud that she was able to keep her voice level. "By Monday."

"Okay," he replied, before picking up his beer bottle from beside him. Regina hadn't even realized he'd put it down, but the memory of his hands on her told her he must have. "Ready to go?"

He didn't sound as though he cared one way or another. Not just as though he didn't want to kiss her again, but as if the kiss hadn't even happened. And here she was, struggling not to turn back into his arms and do it all over again.

"Sure." Hopefully, she matched his indifference.

And she made certain to pull herself together

enough to make light conversation on the way back to her place, although every nerve ending in her body was still vibrating.

She got out of the car as soon as he pulled up outside her building, and he walked with her to the door.

"Thank you for a wonderful evening," he said, causing her to search his expression, which turned out to be unhelpfully neutral.

"Thank you, too." Fishing her keys out of her purse gave her something other than him to concentrate on, and she stiffened when his hand touched her shoulder, and his lips brushed her cheek.

"Good night." His breath was warm against her cheek, and Regina steeled herself not to turn her face and put her lips against his again.

"Good night."

It came out a little breathless, and she stepped away, annoyed, and used her pass card to open the outside door, then walked through without giving him another look.

When she got into the elevator and turned around, he was standing at his open car door, watching her, and even through the glass his gaze caused heat to flare across her chest and back.

CHAPTER SEVEN

MATEO STOOD WAITING for the elevator to go down to the fourth floor the following Thursday, impatiently tapping his toes.

He really shouldn't be this eager to go and see one of his dialysis patients, who'd fallen and been admitted to the hospital, but Rex Knowles was under Regina's care. Mateo hated to admit it, but at this point he was almost desperate for even one glance of the delectable internist.

She'd texted him on Monday, as she said she would, and was as to the point as ever.

I don't think the Keys is going to happen. Thanks for the offer, though.

He'd considered that message for a long time before replying. There were certain responses he was sure would lead to more trouble than they were worth. Asking why was one. Trying to cajole her in some way was another.

He wasn't sure how he was so sure of those

things, but he was. So he took his time thinking it through, before sending her a message.

Offer still stands.

And then he'd taken the two days off anyway.

The way he looked at it was, he had at least a week to try to get her to agree to go to his house on Islamorada, and he was going to give it his best shot.

After the kiss they'd shared, he'd be a damn fool not to.

It had almost blown the top of his head off.

He'd never experienced anything like it, and the memory had haunted him every moment of every day since it happened.

The excitement of having her in his arms, the way her soft, curvy body fitted against his and how it trembled kept him awake at night, tossing and turning, as his brain fed him reminders of her scent and taste.

When she'd pulled back, it was all he could do not to drag her close again, to keep kissing her, touching her, searching out the intimate places to make her as wild as he'd felt.

But then she turned away, cool as a cucumber, and he'd thought she'd been unfazed by their encounter, until he'd seen her fingers tremble. Then he'd known she'd felt it, too.

Of course, how she mentally reacted to the desire crackling between them was another thing altogether, and he didn't think her the type to share her personal thoughts and feelings easily. Getting her to open up about what was happening, or not happening, between them wouldn't be simple. She definitely struck him as a woman who could keep her own counsel.

But if he could get her to discuss the situation, maybe they could have some fun together.

The elevator came, and he stepped in, nodding to the occupants but still lost in his thoughts.

Truth was, Mateo wasn't in the market for a relationship. It didn't feel like the right time for him, although his familial responsibilities had diminished markedly. Even if Regina had relocated to Miami full-time, he couldn't see himself getting involved on any kind of deeper level than the purely physical.

He'd put a lot of his ambitions and plans on hold when his parents died, and was only now in a place where he could start contemplating dusting off and reigniting his goals. While he loved his current job, and hadn't come to a firm decision on whether to move on to something else, it was important to him to have enough space and time to think. In his estimation, getting into a relationship would just be a distraction.

But that didn't preclude a fun, sexy romp with Regina.

If he could just get her to agree.

Getting off on the fourth floor, he spotted the subject of his ruminations at the nurses' station and, ignoring his body's instinctive excited reaction, walked that way.

She looked up and snared him with those lioness eyes. No smile, just a nod in his direction.

"Ah, Dr. Herrera. Your patient, Rexford Knowles, was brought in after falling at home. I need some further information from you."

Just as he expected, she was as cool as cool could be, as though the kiss they'd shared had been erased from her memory. But although that stung, he had to put it all aside.

"He's due in next Tuesday for dialysis," Mateo noted. "What happened?"

Rex Knowles's polycystic kidney disease was at the point where only dialysis was keeping him alive. His wife of almost forty years was looking after him at home with the help of their grown children, but Mateo knew how hard it must be.

"He hasn't been able to tell us exactly how he fell. His daughter stopped by to make him lunch and found him. He was awake but confused, and bleeding from a head wound, so she brought him in. When the ER staff pulled his record, they decided to admit him. My main concern now is for his mental state."

She started walking down the corridor, beckoning Mateo to come along.

"The scalp laceration is over the occipital bone, but there's no apparent fracture of the skull," she continued. "But I saw in your notes that he's been suffering some memory issues recently, and would appreciate you evaluating him. Scans haven't revealed any bleeding or swelling in the brain, but I'm worried about concussion. And with his current polypharmacy, we have to be extra careful."

"His wife was the one who mentioned the memory loss, and I had him evaluated for early-onset dementia, which was ruled out. I suspect it's a direct result of his disease, and the corresponding need for frequent dialysis. He's on the transplant list, but so far, we haven't had any luck finding a match. His wife and all four of his children were tested, but discounted."

She made a little sound, just a soft click of her tongue, which he interpreted as sympathy.

"He hasn't had an episode like this before, has he?"

"Not that I'm aware of, and his wife comes to his appointments to make sure he's telling me everything that's going on. We might need to adjust his blood pressure medication, and I'll do some further testing to see if he's suffering any physical impairment."

She paused at one of the doors and faced him squarely.

"I hope you find him a donor, quickly. Is he on the living donor list, too?"

"Yes. And I know, his condition has been deteriorating far too rapidly for my liking."

She glanced down at the tablet in her hand and scrolled back through the record displayed there. "He's checked regularly for hepatic cysts?"

"Of course. And I'd like copies of the brain scans sent to me, directly. It's just about the time when he's due for an aneurysm check, too."

She nodded, a thoughtful frown creasing her forehead, and then, in a blink, it was gone, and she opened the door.

"Come on," she said, rather abruptly.

And she was through the door and in the room before he could even reach for the handle, leaving him with the sense of having been somehow thoroughly dismissed.

There.

She'd had a totally professional and productive conversation with Mateo without letting on that inside she was a mass of conflicting emotions and longings.

The memory of the kiss they'd shared had

haunted her, springing into her brain whenever she let her defenses down.

If she'd hoped for an indication of whether she was interested enough to pursue anything more with Mateo, she'd gotten more than she'd bargained for. Every night since then, she'd tossed and turned, her imagination supplying brazen, erotic images of what it would be like to see him naked. Feel his mouth and lips and hands on her. Wrap her legs around him, as he filled her to capacity.

It had taken every iota of her considerable strength of will to put it aside and be a decent guest at her cousin's home, but somehow, she'd done it.

But she knew the true test would be how she reacted to Mateo the next time she saw him.

It had been as bad as she'd feared.

She'd sensed him coming down the corridor even before she saw him, some internal sense recognizing the approach of danger, and her entire body had reacted.

Grown hot and tight, thrumming with erotic energy.

Yet, she'd kept it together, and now, watching as Mateo examined Rexford Knowles, asked him questions and checked the test results a nurse had just brought in, she was quietly pleased with herself.

She could do it—put aside the roaring attraction that gripped her whenever she was in his presence, and get on with her job.

Her life.

So confident was she that later, after they'd discussed the patient's ongoing care and Mateo asked her out to dinner that evening, her heart skipped only one beat, instead of fluttering like a crazy thing.

"I'm on call," she said, as a way to get out of it. "And usually do rounds before I head home."

"You'll still have to eat," he replied, his face serious. "I won't be through with my clinic until about six, and usually don't leave until about seven. We could grab a bite after that. I really want to talk to you about the other night."

That was direct. So to the point that she could only reply, "I'm not sure there's anything to discuss."

But she was annoyed to hear the unusually husky tone in her voice, and knew he'd heard it, too, when his eyelids half closed over his gleaming gaze.

"There's a lot to discuss, Regina." Then he half sighed, half snorted, as though unable to decide whether to be annoyed or amused. "Humor me. It's just a sandwich and a conversation."

And because she didn't want him to think she was afraid, she agreed.

By the time she was satisfied with all she wanted to do before she would leave the hospital, it was almost seven thirty, but when she went down to the doctors' parking lot, he was there, waiting. They agreed on an all-night deli near her apartment, and he followed her in his car to the restaurant.

Ensconced in a corner booth, him with a huge Reuben sandwich and her with a cup of soup and a much smaller toasted cheese, they spent the first little while eating.

Obviously, he was as hungry as she was, and it wasn't until he'd finished half of his meal that he wiped his mouth and said, "I wanted you to know, if you don't already, that I'm very attracted to you."

She put down her spoon and met his gaze across the table. It was on the tip of her tongue to tell him she felt the same way about him, but caution, along with her natural reticence, held her back.

"Okay," she said instead, ignoring the fluttering in her belly and her suddenly galloping heart.

"But I also want you to know, in the interest of full disclosure, that as much as I like you and enjoy your company, I'm not interested in a relationship."

Taken aback, all she could do was raise her eyebrows and say, "Oh?"

He nodded. "Besides the fact that you're only here for a short time, the truth is, I've just started to get my life back since my parents passed away. Along with making the commitment to come back to Miami, there were other plans I had to put on hold back then, too. Now I want to try to work on them, before I'm considered too old to make it happen."

That was something she could totally understand, although it felt weird for the shoe to be on the other foot. She was usually the one telling men she wasn't interested in a relationship.

Now she understood why those men had acted so disappointed. Although God knew she didn't plan on getting seriously involved, either, it felt like being rejected.

But she pushed that thought aside to ask, "What are you planning to do?"

"I want to be a part of a dedicated transplant team. There's a new hospital being built near Plantation, and they're rumored to be aiming at being the place to go for chronically ill patients who need transplants. I've applied for some training courses that I hope will put me on track to be a good candidate."

She could see the anticipation and enthusiasm on his face, and couldn't help grinning.

"Good for you."

He leaned back and nodded, but he was serious once more, and she knew her attempt to side-track him from their initial discussion had failed.

"You know by now that I'm not going to try to push you into anything."

"Yes." She made her voice firm, showing with her tone that even if he were so inclined, she was having none of it.

"So, with everything I've said in mind, I'd like to reiterate my invitation to the Keys. No matter what you decide, we'll have a good time."

She took a bite of her sandwich, using the action to put off answering.

He was right. They did have a good time together. Whether or not they decided to take it further, now she knew he wouldn't expect her to get emotionally involved. Best of all, he'd obviously thought it through and was honest about his intentions, or lack of them.

It could be just what she needed: a no-strings, steamy affair, without having to worry about the long-term consequences. They could agree to have fun without expectations, and all without her treating him as though he were a potential life partner.

Weighing and measuring his every move.

Waiting, setting little traps to see what he might do.

Maintaining the tightest grip she could on her own responses and emotions, as though expecting pain at some later, as yet undetermined, date, when their relationship would implode.

None of that was relevant to their situation, and there was no need to be so cagey, when they both knew there would be no long-term relationship to develop and nurture.

And with her track record, wasn't that a great thing?

She could just enjoy herself, without hanging on to all the old habits and norms that had served her so poorly in the past.

Perhaps this was her last chance to experience one of those crazy affairs she'd heard and read about. Not the ones that ended in tears and recriminations, but like those her girlfriends talked about, years after they were over, and both parties had moved on. Where they'd lost their heads for a time, reveling in the hot, steamy sex, and when it was all over, could still sigh and roll their eyes, admitting how good it was, even though it wasn't meant to last.

Regina had never understood why they'd been sucked in, or why the memories still made them fan themselves years later, but she suspected she was about to find out.

Besides, she'd never been to the Keys.

"Can we go to Key West?" she asked, having swallowed. "I want to see Hemingway's house."

"Sure," he replied easily, that sexy little smile

touching the corners of his lips. "Whatever you want."

Whatever she wanted?

That made her brain start churning out suggestions, all of which ended with her having orgasms, and she had to yank it back to the present and slam the door shut on that train of thought.

And while she told herself she probably wouldn't end up sleeping with him, she already knew that was a big fat lie.

"All right. I'll go."

The way his eyes lit up, and the slow, sexy smile he gave her told her he knew just as well as she did that their trip wouldn't be a platonic vacation between friends.

As she finished her sandwich, and the conversation turned more general, she realized she didn't mind being quite so transparent.

CHAPTER EIGHT

IF REGINA STILL harbored any doubts about how wealthy Mateo's family was, they were quickly banished when she saw their house on Islamorada Key.

The modern glass-and-concrete house, set on concrete pillars, was gorgeous.

"They build up high here because of the storm surge during hurricanes," Mateo said. "But my father made sure to use high-impact-resistant glass when he built, and I put on a metal roof when the old one needed to be replaced a few years ago."

Regina was too busy gaping at the breathtaking view out over the water to really pay too much attention to what he was saying, though. She walked from where he'd parked beneath the house out onto the flagstone patio bordered by a little strip of grass, overlooking the sea.

There was a concrete seawall and a hoist holding a tarp-covered boat, but what Regina couldn't stop staring at was the confluence of bright blue sky and aqua-shaded water. All the tension of the last week, when she'd worried about whether to give in to her own desires, melted away.

This wasn't a place where stress could easily survive.

"We're on the Gulf side of the island." Mateo had come to stand beside her, and a little shiver trickled up her back at his presence, so close she could smell his cologne. "So the sunsets are gorgeous. We can go out on the boat one afternoon and watch it, if you like, but unfortunately at this time of year it tends to get dark pretty quickly, so it's a little more difficult coming back in through the channel."

"If that's the case, I'll pass," she said. "I'm sure the view from here is amazing."

The house was part of a development, but it was the last one on the dead-end street and sat on a small peninsula, giving it the perfect position for views on three sides.

"Come on upstairs." Mateo touched her elbow, and goose bumps fired along her arm. "We can put away the groceries, and while you settle in, I'll get the boat in the water."

"Sounds like a plan," she said mildly.

She was determined to play it cool, at least for a little while more. There was a part of her, the suspicious part, that was waiting for him to make the move he'd sworn he wouldn't. Waiting for him to try to force a decision on her, or use the attraction between them to coax her into his bed.

But after they'd unpacked the car, all Mateo did was lead the way upstairs and, after opening the door, usher her inside. As she stood, trying to get her bearings, he carried their bags to the start of a hallway and put them down.

"Pick whichever room you like," he said, waving a hand down the corridor.

Without looking at him, she asked, "Which one is yours?"

"The one at the end of the hall. Make yourself at home."

Then he was out the door again, leaving her to her own devices.

The inside of the house was as lovely as the outside. The large L-shaped room she was standing in was an open-plan kitchen, living and dining room in one, and it was decorated in soothing shades of gray and yellow, accented with crisp white. All the fittings and furnishings had the mark of luxury, but at the same time, it had a comfortable, lived-in feel. Big soft couches and chairs created artful seating arrangements, and were positioned to best take in the glorious view visible through floor-to-ceiling windows.

Kicking off her sandals, Regina carried the bags of groceries she'd brought inside over to the kitchen, and started putting them away. When asked what she should bring, Mateo had said he'd take care of everything, and as she opened the fridge, Regina couldn't help smiling, just a little. Clearly, his idea and her idea of what constituted sufficient provisions for the time they'd be there were very different.

Mind you, he had said he usually ate out when he was in the Keys, so maybe bread, antipasto, cold cuts and enough cheese to make fondue for the entire Swiss population would be enough.

Having finished her chore, she strolled over to the windows, and her gaze immediately went to where Mateo was in the process of turning the winch to get the boat into the water.

The sunlight glinted on his hair, and his broad shoulders bunched and flexed beneath his knit shirt. Watching him without his knowledge was a rare treat, and one she definitely had a taste for.

She already knew where she'd be sleeping, and was honest enough with herself to know she'd made that decision a long time ago. What also had to be acknowledged was the fact that she'd wanted him to push for intimacy, and was strangely disquieted by his refusal to do so.

He'd made his desire for her clear, and had been honest about not being interested in a relationship. Nothing about his behavior should cause her this sense of being on the edge of a precipice and being scared she would plummet with just the slightest push.

Mateo got the boat into the water and began to remove the weatherproof cover, and she saw his lips purse, as though he were whistling. Heat bloomed, low in her belly, and excitement spread through her body, as though pushed along her veins with her blood.

Yes, she was going to sleep with him, and suddenly she realized why she'd wanted him to take the decision from her, the way most men she'd been with had done, or at least tried to.

Then, while she would still have sex with him, her liking and respect for him would be diminished, leaving her free to walk away unscathed when she returned to San Francisco.

Instead, she was forced to admit he was a man of integrity and honor, with a devotion to his family that made her heart ache, and made her like him all the more. And when he'd talked about his ambitions, another piece had clicked into place. How could she not admire both his dedication to his family and his renewed decision to pursue the dreams he'd put on hold all those years ago? Most other people would be resting on their laurels, satisfied with where they were.

She could still remain unscathed, though, as long as she reminded herself that they were both in it for the fun. It was all a matter of determination, and Regina was a master at that, wasn't she?

It would mean keeping a firm grip on her signature detachment, and making sure she didn't let him mess with her head.

No problem at all.

Thus fortified, she went and grabbed her bag, taking it straight along to Mateo's room.

Finished with launching and cleaning up the boat, Mateo stood for a moment, just taking in the view and the peaceful scene. The water was shades of brown where the reefs lay just below the surface, to aquamarine in the shallows, to deep aqua farther out into the Gulf of Mexico. There was little chop, the waves running slow and low toward the land, and the tiny islands dotting the water were verdant green.

While he enjoyed city life, these moments spoke to his soul and eased some of the tension tightening his muscles.

Not all of it, though, because he still wasn't sure where things stood with the gorgeous, tight-lipped, sexy woman upstairs, and the uncertainty was gnawing at his insides.

Her caution didn't bother him; he actually understood it all too well.

There was something brewing between them that threatened to be explosive, and it deserved to be carefully considered before any decisions could be made.

But he'd had to draw on every ounce of patience he possessed not to ask Regina what she was thinking, what she had planned.

He wanted her, and the waiting, the anticipation, intensified not just the need, but his desire to break apart her carefully constructed control. To shatter her detachment and bring her into the eye of the erotic storm building inside. He wanted not just her acquiescence, but her complete complicity. He wanted to ravish her senses, give her the utmost in pleasure, leave her weak but still wanting more.

Where that almost savage impulse came from, he didn't know, but he suspected it had everything to do with this waiting game they were playing.

They'd talked easily on the trip down, the conversation flowing from her visit with her relatives to their separate work ambitions, and then to other, more mundane topics. And while he was engaged, he was also terribly distracted, his senses drawn to cataloging her ever move and breath, her scent filling his head.

The memory of her lips on his, the dance of their tongues, was a constant companion, leading his brain to far more intense and arousing imaginings.

He needed to know which way this situation was going to go, so that if he needed to completely put a lid on his desires, it could happen now.

But standing around outside wasn't going to get him any closer to a resolution, so, with one last comprehensive look at the sky to make sure there were no clouds on the horizon, he turned to go back inside.

Upstairs, he found Regina in the kitchen, putting together lunch.

"Wow," he said, taking in the spread she'd laid out. "You've been busy."

She'd rolled sliced meats and cheeses together, made rosettes out of radishes, and had them all arranged on a platter with celery and carrot sticks, olives and fresh mozzarella balls.

"I'm just toasting some slices of bread," she replied. "And then we can eat."

He went to the sink to wash his hands. "You didn't have to go to so much trouble," he said, thinking about the days when he'd slapped a slice of ham between two slices of bread and called it lunch.

She just smiled. "It was no trouble. Besides, my grandfather always said, 'If yuh mek it look nice-nice, people will nyam it up.' He was a short-order cook with the soul of a chef."

"Okay, I give," he said, amazed at hearing her

speak with a perfect Jamaican accent for the first time, but not wanting to mention how intriguing it was. "I got the rest of it, but what does 'nyam' mean?"

She chuckled. "Eat, but in this context, more like gobble."

He went around to the other side of the counter and sat on one of the stools so he could see her face while they talked.

"Ah... I have to remember that. Micah had a couple of Jamaican friends when he was in high school, and he used to complain that sometimes they'd be talking and he could hardly understand them."

Regina glanced up, amusement making her eyes glitter. "I only ever spoke patois when I was with my grandparents, since my father didn't like to hear it at home. It was fun to sit around with my cousin and her family the other day and hear everybody. Even I had to ask, every now and again, what they were saying. I'm out of practice."

This was a different Regina, he thought. More relaxed and open, and he couldn't help wondering what had changed.

After they'd eaten and put away the leftovers, he said, "How about a boat ride?"

"Sounds like a great idea," she replied, glancing out the window at the bright sunlight. "It looks perfect out there."

"Although it isn't cold, once we get out on the water, the windchill will kick in. Did you bring a windbreaker?"

"I did," she replied, slanting him a sideways glance. "I'll get it as soon as I wash up these dishes."

"Let me do that." He used his hip to gently bump her away from the sink. "You go and get ready."

He couldn't help watching her as she walked away, the delectable sway of her hips a siren's call it took all his strength not to answer.

She hadn't come back by the time he was finished with the dishes, and as he dried his hands, Mateo debated whether to change into his swim trunks or not. The water was too cold to swim in, in his opinion, but you never could tell what could happen when you were out in the ocean. Should an engine fail, or something fall overboard, it would be better to be in his trunks than in jeans.

Heading to his room, he grabbed his bag on the way, idly wondering which of the other four bedrooms Regina had decided on. Which, of course, led to wondering whether he'd be sharing her bed that night.

God, he hoped so. Being around her was driving him a little crazy.

He was three steps into his room, and in the process of putting down his bag on the low bench at the foot of the bed, before his brain caught up to what his eyes had seen.

There was a bag already there.

A gossamer-thin confection of a nightgown lay across the bedspread, and the sandals Regina had been wearing were placed neatly together just in front of the wardrobe.

Frozen where he stood, Mateo looked toward the door of the en suite bathroom, just as Regina strolled out and stopped, five feet away.

She was wearing a bikini, and had her arms raised as she put her hair up into a knot on the top of her head. Meeting his gaze, she raised one eyebrow but didn't try to speak, since she had a hair clip held between her lips.

Mateo couldn't stop his gaze from falling to devour her exposed body, from full breasts, along her toned, curvy body, wide hips, and down her long, strong legs.

In a distant, foggy sort of way, certain other things registered: the silky sheen of her skin, the glint of a diamond in her belly button, the curl of her toes into the rug she was standing on.

Those toes, and the rapid pulse he could clearly see at the base of her throat, were the only indications that Regina was as affected by the moment as he was.

Holding her hair with one hand, she took the clip out of her mouth with the other.

"I hope you don't mind sharing."

Oh, she was trying to sound amused, but the huskiness of her tone gave her away.

"I certainly don't," he replied, not even trying to disguise the desire in his voice. The blood in his veins flowed hot as lava, and he itched to get his hands on her. "In fact, I definitely prefer it this way."

He hadn't consciously made the decision to move but found himself circling her, watching her watch him as he stepped closer, but she didn't move as he stepped behind her. He couldn't get over how sexy she was, how much he wanted to touch her, although he didn't.

Not yet.

"You're so gorgeous it almost hurts to look at you."

The sound she made was one he couldn't recognize.

"I'm glad you think so," she replied.

She seemed to be fumbling a little with the clip, and he realized it was because her hands were shaking. There was a full-length mirror on the other side of the room, and now he looked at her reflection.

"I want to see all of you."

He heard her indrawn breath, saw the way her breasts rose and fell. Letting go of the clip caused her hair to come down, and Mateo gently detangled it from the strands before tossing the clip onto the nearby table.

When he looked back up, she was watching in the mirror, too, and for an instant, he couldn't breathe, ensnared by her gaze. No longer golden, it gleamed dark: a night sky of passion.

She reached behind and untied her top. When it dropped to the floor, Mateo thought he might follow it, felled by the beauty of her naked torso.

Slowly she hooked her fingers into the sides of her bottoms and slid them south, bending to push them past her knees.

Then, as she straightened, euphoria rushed to tighten every muscle in Mateo's body, and for a second, as he stepped closer and ran his finger along her spine, he wondered if he were dreaming.

If so, he hoped he never awoke.

CHAPTER NINE

REGINA TREMBLED AS though about to vibrate right out of her skin. The sensation of Mateo's finger down her spine lingered, a line of fire sending waves of heat cascading out over her entire body, tightening her nipples and making her thighs tremble.

He was standing behind her, watching her reflection in the mirror, and the effect of his gaze on her was electric, sharpening her every sense.

The rush of their breathing was like the wind in a storm.

His scent enveloped her, filling her head like an intoxicant.

Her skin was supersensitized, so that even the slightest movement of the air became a caress.

But what held her totally in thrall was the sight of him, looking at her as though she were the most beautiful woman in the world, his gaze intense and hungry.

Ravenous.

She wanted to see him naked, too, wanted to

tell him to strip down and to kiss her—touch her, alleviate the need building to an explosive pitch inside. To hurry, before she spontaneously combusted. Yet, she was unable to form the words, mute and rooted in place by his eyes.

When he finally touched her again—a light brush of his palms along her arms—she shuddered, closing her eyes to savor the sensation.

"Open your eyes, Regina." The harsh timbre of his voice should have shaken her from her arousal, but instead it pulled her deeper. "I need to see your eyes."

She obeyed, and the clash of their gazes made a moan rise in her throat.

Then it was the sight of his hands sliding around to cup her breasts, coupled with the slip of flesh on flesh, that brought her up onto her toes.

It was torture of the most erotic kind, and Regina watched it play out as Mateo skillfully, masterfully took her higher in excruciating increments.

He touched her as though he were learning every inch of her skin through his fingertips. As his thumbs circled her nipples, he set his lips to her neck, and the flick of his tongue echoed across her system, setting off tremors with each pass.

Lower those wicked hands went, and she

watched, hardly blinking, as they inched closer to that aching, needy space between her thighs. One touch would send her over the edge. She was sure of it, and craved that contact in a way she'd never desired anything in her life before.

But he withheld that intimacy, caressing her belly, the top of her thighs, her hips and buttocks.

Why didn't she grab his hand and take it to where she wanted it to be? That was what she'd usually do. But somehow with Mateo, as desperately as she wanted culmination, she couldn't bring herself to demand it.

There was something so erotic about his total concentration on her body, and the sight of them together, that all she could do was keep watching.

And feeling.

The slide of hands, and the slip of his mouth across her nape.

The brush of his fingers on her mound, and the scrape of his teeth on her neck.

Tender circles around her tingling nipples.

Just when she thought she couldn't take a moment more, he turned her a quarter turn, stepping around to kiss her, and the passion between them became a flashover.

Where before he'd been slow, each touch filled with intent, now they strained against each other, the wanting driving them to rush.

But although the pace had increased, Mateo

never relinquished control. When she tried to undress him, he ignored her efforts, dipping his head to take one straining nipple between his lips.

Regina arched back over the arm he banded around her waist, and it was probably the only thing keeping her upright on her quaking legs. Tunneling her fingers into his hair, she drowned in the moment.

Then his lips were sliding down her body, his hands hard and tight on her ass, keeping her on her feet even as he sank to his knees. When he lifted her leg and put it over his shoulder, Regina was already just a breath away from orgasm.

And the first touch of his tongue was all she needed to achieve it.

She cried out, a sound she'd never heard herself make before in her life, and held his head there, although he'd made no effort to shift away.

She rode out the crashing waves, feeling him still as the final tremors shook her to the core. But before she could catch her breath, he did something wicked-sweet with his mouth, and she was tumbling into another, even harder release.

How had she gotten onto the bed? she wondered, when she finally recovered enough to open her eyes, and found herself lying on the smooth, cool comforter.

Mateo was taking off his clothes, and her

body—which had seemed draped in lethargy a second before—tingled back to life at the sight.

Bronze skin stretched over the hard, well-defined muscles of his chest and abdomen, making her want to dig her nails into them and test their strength. A trail of dark hairs led down toward the top of his jeans, and she resolved, there and then, to follow it as soon as possible, with her mouth.

Her breath caught in her throat when he stood up from shucking his pants.

He was, she thought in a distant, stupefied sort of way, ridiculously beautiful.

"You're so sexy," she said, the words falling unbidden from her lips.

Mateo paused, his eyebrows going up as though in surprise, before he replied, "I was just thinking the same thing about you."

She held out her arms, ravenous for him, and when he lowered himself to the bed, there was no need for further conversation.

Their bodies did the talking for them.

And boy, did his have a lot to say.

Hers responded with a series of mind-blowing orgasms. More than should be legal, she thought through the fog of endorphins rampaging in her system. By the time he finally rolled on a condom, she was almost desperate for his possession.

But once again, Mateo surprised her.

He'd been in complete control of her body up until that point, but now he yielded to Regina, pulling her to straddle his hips. Letting her set the pace, and take over.

It was a powerful and somehow empowering moment.

To kneel above him and watch his face tighten with pleasure as she took him deep energized her all over again.

She wanted to make him as crazy as he'd made her, but the moment was too sublime to prolong, and her need was too great. And it didn't take long for her to find release again, but this time she pulled him along with her, and her ecstasy was heightened by his.

Lying beside him, tucked under his arm, Regina yawned, cataloging all the yummy little aches popping up all over her body. Having sex with Mateo had turned out to be better than any cardio workout she'd ever done.

"Tired?"

She shook her head. "No. Although I feel as though I should be, after what we just did."

He chuckled. His arm, which was around her shoulders, tightening just a little. Regina couldn't help wondering if now that they'd slept together, he'd expect them to spend the rest of the trip in bed.

Not that she'd complain. After this first taste,

she was more than willing to gorge herself on Mateo's brand of loving. Night shift be damned. The day shift had turned out to be more than satisfactory, and she suspected any shift at all in his bed would be equally mind blowing, if not more so.

But at the same time, it would be nice to see more than just the inside of his house.

As though reading her mind, Mateo said, "I thought we could go to Key West tomorrow. If we leave in the morning, we could stop and get breakfast on the way there, and then explore to your heart's content for the rest of the day."

"Sounds good." Well, that answered her question. "How long does it take to get there?"

"About two hours."

His hand was gently rubbing up and down her arm, and Regina found herself deliciously distracted. Maybe staying all afternoon in his bed wouldn't be such a bad idea.

"Do you want to go out on the boat? There's enough light left for us to go out into the Gulf for a quick run."

His hand was on her shoulder now, just in line to slip down and cup her breast, if he wanted to. She wanted him to, but somehow also didn't want to admit it and appear as though she was getting addicted to him.

"Sounds good," she said, but neither of them moved. Not for a couple of long, drugged beats.

And then he rolled over and kissed her, and she knew it would be a while before they went out on the water.

Mateo went down to the dock while Regina got ready to go for their boat ride. As he checked the gas gauges, he found himself whistling, and abruptly stopped, trying to figure out what it was he was feeling.

Satiated? Sure.

He couldn't tell when last he'd experienced that level of arousal and satisfaction—if he ever had before.

But there was something else making him grin to himself and start whistling once more.

Recognizing it as happiness didn't feel right, so he pushed the sensation to the back of his mind.

When she came down, she was wearing a windbreaker and had put a scarf over her hair. Since he was finished checking the boat, they set off right away.

As he navigated out through the narrow channel, Regina stood beside him, taking in the changing vistas as they moved farther from shore. Normally, he'd have one or more of the kids with him, or be alone, but having her there felt good. Natural.

Once out into the wider channel, he said, "Hold on tight," then opened up the throttle to put the boat up on a plane. As they flew across the water, cutting through the waves, Regina let out a whoop, making Mateo check to see if it was an expression of fear or one of enjoyment.

With her head thrown back, she was holding on to her scarf and laughing, clearly thrilled. He'd never seen her like that before, exhibiting such unfettered emotion, and the sight of it set something free inside him, too. Something hot and wild and possessive.

He had to force himself to turn away, to concentrate on what he was doing and where he was steering the boat.

He passed one of the mangrove islands, and ahead was open water, so he upped the speed a bit more, until the wave heights began to increase, causing the boat to bounce more than he considered comfortable. Throttling back, he brought the boat down to idle, letting it drift and rock.

Turning to face Regina, he found himself the focus of her attention, and even behind her dark glasses, he could tell her eyes were sparkling.

"That was amazing," she said with a wide

grin. "I haven't been on a boat in ages. I'd forgotten how much fun it can be."

The flash of jealousy firing through him was insane and ridiculous, but it took all of Mateo's control not to ask her who else she'd been boating with. He wanted to take hold of her and kiss her, and make sure she remembered no other boat ride than the one she was on with him.

But he said and did neither, just smiled at her and said, "We could stay here for a little while, or we can go farther out. It's up to you."

She walked out from beneath the T-top to the rear deck and stood there looking out across the water. She unzipped her windbreaker and shrugged it off, lifting her face to the sun.

"Let's stay here," she said finally. "It's so peaceful."

They were the only vessel in sight, and the tide was pushing them away from the nearest land, so Mateo didn't bother to drop anchor. Stepping to the side, away from the wheel, he leaned back against the console, watching Regina.

She had on a pair of form-fitting terry cloth yoga pants and a loose knit shirt, all of which showed off her luscious figure to perfection. When she bent over to look down into the water, Mateo's body tightened, and his hands itched to cup her gorgeous butt and squeeze.

When she straightened and turned, Mateo

tightened his grip on the console, to restrain himself from beckoning her near and begging for more of the closeness he craved so badly.

She froze, and time seemed to waver and stretch as they stared at each other. Then she strode across the deck to him, and she was where he so desperately wanted her to be.

Back in his arms.

She was irresistible, setting off a fire in his blood as soon as those lioness eyes turned on him. The memories of her responses as they made love had him desperate to do it all over again, just so he could see her shatter in his arms.

The exhilaration of their race across the water still thrummed through his veins, and it seemed to have aroused her, too, and she kissed him as though for the first time, leaving no doubt as to her intent.

They'd agreed it was all just for fun—for the physical enjoyment—but when he had her in his arms, it felt bigger. As though there was something growing between them, tying him to her in some fundamental way.

But he didn't hesitate when she walked into his personal space. His arms went around her, pulling her flush against his chest, and he parted his legs so that she stood between them, showing her without words that she wasn't the only one revved up.

Then he kissed her, putting all his need and conflicting emotions into the embrace. She felt so right in his arms, and when she swiveled her hips, he groaned into her mouth.

Her hands roamed his back and then his chest. When she pushed them up under his shirt and slid the pads of her fingers across his straining muscles, desire overtook him.

Placing his hands on her bottom, he lifted her and stepped forward. Instinctively her legs came up to wrap around his waist, and he felt her shudder as her core came into contact with his erection.

Putting her down on the edge of the captain's seat, he broke their kiss to trail his lips down to her throat. Regina arched, giving him full access to her neck. When his teeth scraped along the skin and he followed it with a hot swipe of his tongue, he heard her gasp and felt her tremble.

There.

There was the responsiveness that made him lose his mind and want to make her come over and over again. She was the stuff of every erotic fantasy he'd ever had, and he was willing to lose himself in her arms again, as long as he didn't lose himself in the process.

There was no future between them, he knew, just the present, and he wanted to gorge himself on her while he had the chance.

She tightened her legs around his waist and arched her back even more, offering her breasts to his lips.

He didn't hesitate.

Pushing her blouse up, he slipped her bikini top aside to suck her already straining nipple between his lips. She moaned, her hips swiveling, and Mateo growled. A sound broke through the fog in his head, and he drew back.

She protested, but he was already smoothing her shirt down, as disappointed as she seemed to be at the interruption.

"Company is coming," he said.

When she became aware of the fast-approaching engine, he saw a wave of color flood her face, but she laughed.

"They're a little late," she said as she took the hand he held out to help her get down off the chair, and then reached under her blouse to adjust her swimsuit. "They missed the show."

Seeing her amusement just made him want her even more, so he didn't answer, just scooped her back into his arms and kissed her until her breath was once more rushing from her lungs.

It was only when the passing boaters cheered that he let her go, and said, "That's it. We're heading home."

She laughed again, and he had to force himself to turn back to the console and get the engines going.

The ride back seemed to take an inordinate amount of time, and by the time they docked, anticipation was like lava in his veins.

All he could hope was that he wouldn't become too addicted to Regina Montgomery, because the craving he had for her was already intense.

CHAPTER TEN

THE WEEKEND SEEMED to fly by, a whirl of sight-seeing, boat trips and lovemaking.

Especially lovemaking.

Regina had realized at one point—probably as they sat in a restaurant on Duval Street in Key West, discussing everything and nothing—that she was a little afraid. Not of Mateo—not in the slightest—but of the sensation of being ever so slightly out of control, no matter how hard she tried to reassure herself she could handle whatever came.

But she pushed it all aside, and now, as they drove back into Miami, she was sorry their time together was already coming to an end.

Mateo apparently felt the same way.

"Would you like to stay at my place tonight? I can drop you home before I go to work in the morning."

Oh, she was tempted, but her natural caution reasserted itself, after apparently having taken the weekend off. If it had been firmly in place, surely Regina wouldn't have lost her head quite as completely as she had under Mateo's spell.

"I really have to take care of all the things I usually do on weekends," she said, trying to sound matter-of-fact but hearing the regret in her own voice. "I like to start the week with all my chores done, and of course this week that hasn't happened."

She was getting used to his way of not pressuring her, so it came as no surprise when he replied, "I understand. Maybe later in the week, before you start back up on shift?"

"Maybe." It was the most she was willing to agree to. Right now, she needed a little distance from him so she could think through everything that had happened over the weekend.

It turned out to be a good decision, as she was called in the following morning to cover for the internist on duty, who'd had a personal emergency and had to go out of town.

Regina was glad to be back at work, since she'd tossed and turned all the night before, obsessively going over everything that had happened over the weekend.

No man had ever made her feel the way Mateo had, and not just physically. There was something about the way he looked at her and listened so intently that drilled down into her soul. It was the demeanor of a man completely involved in the moment, not waiting to speak, or thinking about what would happen next.

No, he was totally there, in a way she wasn't used to but knew she could, all too easily, grow accustomed to.

Thank goodness she wasn't contemplating any more long-term relationships in the future, because any man she was involved in would have to put up with being compared with Mateo.

Both in and out of bed.

And she couldn't stop thinking about the "in bed" part, and that was an anomaly for her, since she'd never allowed sex to mess with her head. It was fun, and something she was completely comfortable with, but not an activity she built any part of her life around. Too many men seemed ready to use their sexual prowess as a way to control their partners, and Regina was having none of it.

But if she were inclined to be controlled that way, Mateo would definitely be in the running for puppet master. That man knew his way around a woman's body.

Realizing she was woolgathering again, Regina pulled herself together and started her rounds. Looking over the charts of newly admitted patients, she had a momentary jolt of annoyance when she realized she'd be dealing with

Dr. Welk. The pompous cardiologist was truly aggravating.

Then she took a closer look at the young woman's chart and found herself wondering exactly what was going on.

According to Kaitlyn Mignon's medical history, she'd suffered from a variety of nonspecific symptoms for most of her life, but she hadn't been definitively diagnosed with any one illness that could take all of them into consideration.

Stomach complaints. Intermittent fevers. Fatigue and frequent headaches.

What had caused her to be admitted to the hospital was her doctor's suspicion that she'd suffered a series of transient ischemic attacks, which often were a precursor to a stroke. Although the symptoms—in her case an inability to see—had resolved within a few minutes, the doctor had wanted her to undergo further testing, including being on a heart monitor.

Her test results had shown signs of a possible heart valve abnormality, which was why Dr. Welk was on the case. But what caught Regina's eye was another result, which indicated proteinuria.

There was something on the edge of Regina's brain, nagging at her, but until she could get to a computer station and do some research, the only other thing she could do was call for a nephrology consult.

Somewhere in the confluence of all those symptoms lay an answer, and she was determined to find it.

Having called up Nephrology and being told Dr. Linton would be down in a short time, Regina went on about her rounds, somewhat thankful she wouldn't have to see Mateo just yet.

She couldn't help thinking it would be good to have a little more time before she encountered him, just to make sure she was prepared.

A couple of hours later, Regina was passing the nurses' station on her way to another patient's room, when the nursing supervisor, Lisa Patterson, stopped her.

"Dr. Montgomery, can I have a minute?"

"Sure. What's up?"

The supervisor looked around at the other doctors and nurses in the vicinity, and then said in a low voice, "Can we go somewhere quieter?"

That was never a good sign, but Regina nodded and followed the other woman to the enclosed office space behind the main station.

Lisa closed the door and then said, "There's a situation that came to my attention, and I want you to know about it."

"What is it?"

"Dr. Linton came down from Nephrology, as

you asked, but I understand Dr. Welk told him he wasn't needed."

"Oh?"

Despite the mildness of her response and her poker face, she was sure Lisa knew that inside she was livid.

That blasted Welk.

"I wasn't there, but the nurse who was present reported it to me, and I thought you should know."

"Yes, thank you. I appreciate the heads-up."

They exited the room together, Regina's brain racing to figure out how best to handle the situation.

Morgan Welk, she'd come to learn, acted like the lord of the manor because of his long tenure at the hospital, and especially loved to boss around the younger, less confident doctors. Unfortunately, Mark Linton was one of the newest members of the nephrology team, and clearly didn't know how to stand up to a bully like Welk.

Well, Regina was about to show him how.

Back at the nurses' desk, she looked up the extension for Nephrology and put in a call.

"Dr. Linton, please. This is Dr. Montgomery."

"I'm sorry, Dr. Montgomery, but Dr. Linton is in with a patient just now. Can anyone else help you?"

Regina only just stopped herself from grimacing. She'd really wanted to turn the situation into a teaching moment for the young doctor, but she couldn't leave her patient up in the air waiting for him.

"Is there another doctor available?"

"Dr. Herrera is here. Shall I page him for you?"

Her heart fluttered.

"Yes, thank you," she replied, keeping her voice cool, masking her less than professional response. She'd been sure he would be working in the clinic, which was held twice a week for the patients with chronic kidney disease, so she hadn't expected to have to speak with him.

Knowing she was going to have to interact with him here, at the hospital, caused a rush of excitement through her system, and brought to mind all kinds of naughty memories.

And that annoyed her almost as much as Welk's actions.

So her voice was curt when he came on the line and she replied to his greeting.

"Mateo, I have a situation here, and I need someone from your department to attend, stat."

There was a pause, and then he replied, "I can be down in about ten minutes. Will that do?"

"Yes, thank you."

She hung up before he could say anything more, and after she'd given the nurse on duty some instructions regarding the last patient she'd seen, she sat at one of the monitors and began her research.

Mateo wasn't sure what he was in for when he got down to the fourth floor.

Regina's voice had been curt and cold, and he knew something had gone wrong; he just wasn't sure where, or what.

Hopefully, that tone was directed at the problem, rather than him personally.

He should have known that whatever was bothering her would be professionally related. Regina would never allow her personal life to interfere with work.

"Fabry disease?" Mateo said it slowly, turning it over in his head. He looked back at the tablet she'd given him, scrolling up to the section with the patient's history. "Wouldn't it have been diagnosed long before this? According to her chart, she's been exhibiting symptoms for years."

Regina swung her chair around to point at the screen.

"It says that up until the early 2000s many doctors considered females with the genetic anomaly to be strictly carriers. I'm willing to guess not many doctors, even today, are well versed on it, or would even think of it in regard to a female patient."

"That's probably true." Kaitlyn had been diagnosed with irritable bowel syndrome, migraines and a host of other illnesses, but no one had put it together.

Until now.

"I'm going to order the genetic test, if she's amenable, but I need your input for treatment going forward. I also have an issue with Morgan Welk that you should be aware of."

"Oh?" Just hearing that man's name got his back up, and when Regina explained what had happened earlier, he was furious.

"I'll speak to Linton," he said. "And to Welk. If it had come out that you'd called for a consult, and no one had examined the patient, our department would be in a lot of trouble."

"Leave Welk to me," she said with a thin smile. "I'll deal with him myself."

If Mateo hadn't been so angry, he'd feel bad for the cardiologist, but as it was, all he said was, "Go get him, tiger."

Her lioness eyes flashed with grim amusement. "I shall."

Mateo cast a quick glance behind him, and finding the area clear, said quietly, "Come by later?"

Regina shook her head. "No, sorry. I'm on call for the next couple of days, and I never socialize when on duty."

"So you'll be working these shifts, as well as your seven?"

She shrugged. "They haven't worked it all out yet, but they think Dr. Reynolds will be back by Thursday, and if he is, he'll work my weekend shifts and we'll get back on track that way."

"If that's the case, let's do something on the weekend."

He didn't want to sound as though he was needy, but he really wanted to see her away from the hospital, and was very aware of her time in Miami marching far too quickly on.

"Sure." She didn't sound terribly enthusiastic, but the look she gave him out of the corner of her eye sent a trickle of heat along his spine. "I'll let you know what's happening."

Then they went to see the patient, who appeared equal parts tired, afraid and angry.

"Okay, *another* doctor?" She eyed Mateo with patent distrust. "I hope at least this one has some manners. That old guy is an asshole."

Mateo bit back a snort of agreement and introduced himself, explaining that her urine analysis indicated there may be some disruption in her kidney function.

"I'd like to do some further tests, if that's okay with you."

Kaitlyn Mignon flushed, and cursed long and hard. Both Regina and Mateo instinctively moved closer to the head of the bed, and Mateo saw Regina reach for the nearby box of tissues.

"My kidneys, now, too? What next? I can't stand it anymore."

"I know," Regina said in that cool, controlled tone that seemed to cut right through to the heart of the matter, but this time all it gained her was a glare and another string of curses.

"You have *no idea*. Every time I turn around, it's something new. Something different, and worse. I can't lead a normal life like everyone else, and there's no answers as to why this is happening."

"We—Dr. Herrera and I—we think you may have a genetic disorder called Fabry disease. That's why we want to do further tests."

Kaitlyn stared at Regina, her mouth agape, and Mateo realized why Regina had grabbed a handful of tissues, when the first tear trickled down the younger woman's cheek.

"You…you think you know what's…wrong with me?" Her hushed tone was such a marked contrast to her previous outbursts it showed how stunned she was by the thought. "Is there a cure?"

"There is no cure, but there are therapies that may help you, if you qualify for them. Otherwise, it's a matter of treating the symptoms and managing the disease in a variety of ways."

Kaitlyn was still staring at Regina, and then she burst into sobs.

It took a while for Kaitlyn to regain her composure, and when she did, her breath was still hitching in her throat as she said, "Just to have some kind of answer to why I've had these symptoms and problems all my life would be a relief."

"It's not a certainty," Mateo said, wanting to manage her expectations. "We'd have to do molecular genetic testing for the mutated GLA gene to be absolutely sure, but your history does seem to point that way."

They were discussing it further with her when Dr. Welk walked into the room. He froze, as though unable to believe his eyes.

Before he could say anything, though, Regina went from cool comforter of the sick to ice-cold avenger.

"Dr. Welk." The frost dripping from her voice seemed to push the temperature in the room down by ten degrees. "May I have a word with you, outside?"

It wasn't really a question, and even Welk seemed compelled to follow her as she strode out the door.

Kaitlyn Mignon watched them go, and although her eyes were red and swollen, and her nose was pink, Mateo saw the amusement in her expression.

"Wouldn't want to be that guy," she muttered. "Dr. Montgomery looks *pissed*."

"Yep," he agreed. "I wouldn't want to be him, either."

But, oh, how he wanted to be the man who once more melted that ice and had her crying out in ecstasy.

Regina's brand of loving was addictive, and he wanted as much of it as he could get.

CHAPTER ELEVEN

WHAT SHE'D TOLD Mateo was the truth. She never socialized when on call.

Yet by Wednesday morning, she was absolutely contemplating breaking her own rule and inviting Mateo over that evening.

The night before, for the first time that she could remember, she'd felt lonely. Adrift, as though some essential mooring had been slipped over the weekend with Mateo, and she was floating without a destination.

Ridiculous, of course. Her destination was still as fixed as it had ever been—perhaps even more so, since she'd received an email from the hospital in San Francisco, announcing the retirement of the current Chief of Medicine. He'd finally set a date of departure, which was six months hence.

She'd known the retirement was in the works for a while, and that the hospital board had already chosen the Deputy Chief to replace him. It wasn't her time quite yet, but she'd positioned herself to keep moving up in the hierarchy, and was hopeful that all her hard work would pay off with a promotion to the next level.

Then she'd be third from the top, behind whoever was chosen as Deputy Chief of Medicine.

Although it seemed as if her plans and hard work were paying off, she'd felt no real excitement on seeing the email, and no amount of telling herself she *should* be excited helped.

She'd wanted to call Mateo and tell him about it, so as to get a relatively unbiased view of it all, but that wasn't the kind of relationship they had.

More like, not the kind of relationship she *wanted* to have with him.

There was no future in being his friend, or considering him hers. No use in cultivating the kind of relationship where his opinion and advice were important. That hearkened back to her mother having to take her father's "advice" before doing even the simplest of things, and just thinking about it made Regina's stomach curdle.

She'd thought about calling Cher, just for a chat, but had gotten lost in the memories of the weekend spent with Mateo, and then realized it was too late to phone her friend, who went to bed with the birds.

That had left her with only her muddled thoughts and physical yearnings for company.

It was no good telling herself that she didn't want to want Mateo the way she did, when every nerve ending in her body was set on reminding her of how good he made her feel. So here she was, trying to figure out which was better: another sleepless night of tossing and turning with unfulfilled desire, or setting a precedent she'd probably regret.

She chose the latter, rationalizing that she couldn't go on suffering insomnia and still being her usual effective self at work.

Mateo was the cure for what ailed her.

Besides, it was a carefully considered action, she reassured herself, rather than a spur-of-the-moment loss of control. Wanting to have a physical urge taken care of was natural, and when it could be easily dealt with, and out of the way, there was no need to quibble.

Although tempted to text him, she called instead, from her private phone to his, but had to leave a message.

He called her back thirty minutes later.

"Hi, what's up?" he asked when she answered.

She walked a little way away from the desk, for privacy.

"I was wondering if you—"

"Yes," he said, before she could finish.

Regina couldn't help the gurgle of laughter that bubbled up in her throat.

"You don't know what I was going to ask."

"I don't care. For you, anything."

For some reason that went straight to her heart, and warmth radiated out from that silly organ.

It almost made her change her mind, but she found herself saying, "Come by later?"

"What time?"

She glanced at the desk. It had been a busy day, and she didn't know when it would end.

"Is nine too late?"

"Not at all. See you then."

And she spent the rest of the day with a strange floaty sensation making her want to smile at everyone she met.

Except Dr. Welk, who was intent on treating her as though she was something he'd found on the bottom of his shoe, because of her giving him what-for the day before.

Just thinking about his behavior made her shake her head. He'd been adamant that Kaitlyn Mignon wasn't suffering from Fabry disease, and that they were wasting time and money in testing her for the condition.

"She has a heart valve abnormality and is suffering from TIAs, and that's all there is to it. All this other mucking about is making my treatment of the patient more difficult."

Regina had kept the smile on her face with a great deal of effort.

"Since she's my patient at this time, and I've done exhaustive research into her prior history, it's my professional opinion that Fabry disease accounts for all the diverse symptoms she's experienced over her life."

"Fabry's is only symptomatic in males. Don't you know that?"

"Research has proven otherwise." Disgusted, she'd added, for good measure, "In fact, it's been more than fifteen years since it became common knowledge that females with Fabry's can also be symptomatic, and not just carriers. You really should keep up-to-date on the current research, Dr. Welk."

Apparently, that had been too much for him, and he'd walked away.

Regina was still surprised she hadn't gotten a call from Administration or Human Resources, as she was sure he wasn't going to let it go. Hopefully, the genetic test results would put the entire situation to rest.

And in the meantime, she had tonight to look forward to, and that made the rest of the day seem like an eternity.

She got home just twenty minutes before Mateo was slated to arrive, and dashed into the shower to wash off the workday. When the doorbell rang, she was still wrapped in a towel, with nothing else on, and a wicked impulse had her pushing the buzzer to let him in just the way she was.

His expression, when she opened the apartment door, made the decision a great one. Just the way his face tightened and his eyes grew dark had her arousal soaring.

He kicked the door closed behind him, just as she gave the towel a tug and it dropped to the floor.

"I've been thinking about this all damn day," he growled, reaching to trace a finger along her throat, and down to her already puckered nipple. "No, that's a lie. I've been thinking about you since the moment I dropped you off on Monday."

Again, that ridiculous warm feeling blossomed in her chest, and she held out her arms.

"Here I am."

They didn't make it farther than the couch.

It seemed he was as ravenous for her as she was for him, and Regina let all the fears about what they were getting into be blown away on the waves of the ecstasy crashing through her body.

They finally made it to her bed about an hour after Mateo had first arrived, and he set about making love to Regina again.

Afterward, as she lay cuddled alongside him, he wondered how, in such a short period of time, he'd become so attached to her.

He hadn't been lying when he said he'd thought

about her constantly since they parted. Somehow she'd gotten into his blood, and he was beginning to think he'd never get enough of her.

But it was also clear that she was just in it for the sex, and that wasn't something he could complain about, since he'd been the one to set the rules of engagement.

No relationship, just fun.

Well, it was all fun and games until feelings started getting involved, and he was pretty sure it was edging past that stage for him already.

He wasn't going to bring any of that up with her, though. Not with the chance that she'd completely shut him out, and their relationship—such as it was—would end sooner than it had to.

"I got an email from my job in San Francisco."

Her sudden words startled him. He thought she'd fallen asleep.

"Oh? What was it about?"

She was quiet for a moment and then said, "The current Chief of Medicine is retiring. I knew he'd been talking about it for a while, but I didn't know when it would happen."

The sensation running through him was a confluence of conflicting emotions, but he pulled his excitement for her to the forefront.

"Do you think you'll be offered his position?"

The sound she made was a cross between a huff of amusement and a snort.

"No, I'm not there yet. I doubt I'm even in the running for the Deputy spot, but it's all getting closer."

He tried to put himself in her shoes, to figure out the parameters under which she was working toward her goal.

"How do they fill those top-tier positions?" he asked. There were varying protocols at different hospitals. "Is it a board decision alone, based on current staff, or by applications?"

"It's usually a board decision, unless there's no one they're willing to promote, but I don't think they have that problem. The current Deputy is slated to be promoted, and I'm almost sure I know who he'll want for his second. All I can hope is that I'm next in line."

Mateo squeezed her shoulders.

"You'll get there. Is there any way to up your chances further?"

She seemed to think about that for a little while, and then sighed.

"I'm pretty sure I've done all I can. No one has faulted my work. I've had no malpractice suits filed against me, or complaints to the board, except for the one doctor who expressed the opinion that I was too sharp with my colleagues." She chuckled. "My defense was that he was too thin-skinned, and the board seemed to agree with me."

"Well, then, unfortunately all you can do is wait."

She rolled over so her hands rested on his chest, and they were face-to-face.

"I don't want to wait. I've worked toward this for so long, and it feels as though it's almost as far away as it was six years ago."

He shook his head, raising his hand to caress her cheek.

"But you know it isn't as far away, and that you've put in the work to get to where you want to, and that's really all you can do."

With a sigh, she nodded. "I know, but I can almost taste it, you know?"

He did know. Fulfilling her goal was of paramount importance to her, and it was eating at her that it was still out of reach.

"Hey, you've come too far to be discouraged. Especially now, when there's some movement in the hierarchy." Then it struck him. "Wait, are you worried that they won't move you up a level when the current Chief leaves?"

Her eyes were shadowed as she replied, "It has occurred to me, although I haven't allowed myself to think about it too much. The reality is, there aren't a lot of women in those higher positions, and only one other African American, who's the Deputy Chief of Surgery, and male.

My chances, based on those conditions, aren't that good."

Mateo sought the right words. It wasn't an easy conversation to have, and he wasn't willing to either dismiss her fears, or try to diminish their veracity.

"I think…" he said slowly, trying to gather his thoughts, "I think you're right to consider those circumstances, and wonder if your sex and race might hold you back. We both know the possibility exists. But I also know that no one works harder than you do, or has a better rapport with patients, and you're one of the best diagnosticians I've worked with. I mean, who else would look at a case like Kaitlyn Mignon and put all the clues together that way?"

"I'm sure there are lots of other doctors who would," she replied, but she sounded more relaxed, as though his words were getting through to her.

"Maybe, but I'm telling you, you're special, and really great at what you do. Plus, you've expanded your qualifications beyond what might otherwise be expected, all while carrying a full workload. You've done your part, and if the hospital doesn't appreciate what they have in you, they're idiots."

Leaning forward, she kissed him. It was just

a brief, soft touch of her lips to his, but it filled him with warmth and longing.

Not sexual longing, but the kind of longing that made his arms tighten around her and never want to let go.

Then she smiled, her face lighting up, eyes gleaming, and he knew he was falling for her even as he fought against it, knowing it would lead only to heartbreak.

"You're very good for my ego," she said, resting her cheek against his chest.

"I'm not trying to be," he pointed out. "It's all the truth."

Before she could answer, her phone rang.

"Dammit," she muttered, rolling away to answer it. "Regina Montgomery."

Mateo listened to her side of the conversation, and knew, even before she hung up, that she would be heading back to the hospital.

He got up, looking around for his clothes, then remembered they were in the living room.

"Oh," she said, after hanging up. "I meant to tell you, Paul Reynolds will be back on shift on Friday, which means I'm off for the weekend."

"Great. How about a trip over to St. Petersburg? I think you'd like it."

"Sure," she said. She was still naked, hunting in the closet for something, and Mateo cursed the hospital for calling her in. He would have happily spent the night holding her close, instead of going back to his lonely bed. "That sounds good."

"And the weekend after, it's my birthday. I'm having a little party, and I'd really like you to come."

That had her turning around to look at him, and her gaze was extra-searching, as though she was trying to figure out why he'd want her there.

"Will your family be there?"

"Yes," he replied, trying to keep his tone casual. There was no way he wanted her to know just how eager he was to introduce her to his siblings, and see how they interacted.

Although his head was telling him not to get too involved, his heart had other plans.

After what seemed like forever, she nodded. "I'd like that."

And he felt as though he could once more breathe.

When they were both dressed and ready, they left at the same time, and he kissed her lightly inside the elevator, since her car was parked in the secure underground lot, and his was outside.

"Stay safe," he told her, making her smile.

"Have a good night," she replied as he got out of the elevator and she continued down another floor.

Driving home, Mateo tried to sort through his

emotions but couldn't. They were too tangled up and confused. The one thing he was able to decide on was the fact that, with Regina, he was having the time of his life, and he resolved to enjoy it as much as he possibly could, for as long as it lasted.

He'd put off living his life for too long to complain about this new, exciting chapter not being exactly what he would have hoped for.

And he knew all too well that nothing lasted forever.

It made sense to keep reminding himself of that, even while he sought out pleasure in Regina's company.

CHAPTER TWELVE

ST. PETERSBURG WAS GORGEOUS, but the weekend flew by, leaving her vaguely melancholy. Her time with Mateo had already begun to wane, like the moon. But unlike that celestial body, their relationship wouldn't rise, full and beautiful, again.

They walked on the windswept beach, visited the Dalí Museum and the Chihuly exhibit, where Regina found herself dazzled by the art glass installations. This was an experience unlike any she'd had before: magical and transformative. The colors and shapes seemed to swirl and dance, leading her into a trancelike state that lasted until well after they'd left.

At lunch, she was still quieter than usual, leading Mateo to ask, "You really loved the glass exhibit, didn't you?"

His smile did something to her insides, adding to the sensation of being someone slightly different than she'd always been.

"I don't have the words to describe how I feel about it," she admitted.

He didn't reply, just offered her his hand across the table. She took it, her gaze locked with his, and it was then she realized why his expression affected her the way it did.

It was the same way he looked when he spoke about his family—his parents and siblings, the life they'd all had together. That tender set of his mouth, the soft crinkling of the skin at the corners of his eyes were indicative of some sweet emotion she knew she had no right to.

Drawing her hand away was instinctive, and far harder than she cared to admit even to herself, but was the right thing to do. They'd agreed to the parameters, and either of them getting attached would negate the whole point of their relationship and cause far more problems than either of them wanted.

On the way back to Miami on Sunday evening, she asked, "What should I bring to the party next Saturday? And how fancy is it going to be?"

"It's casual, and you don't need to bring anything. Lola and Cristóbal are flying in on Thursday, and they're in charge of putting it all together. It'll be maybe twenty people, at the most."

It would be interesting to see him interacting with his brothers and sisters, but at the same time, she had to admit to being a little nervous, and torn about whether she really wanted to go or not.

Theirs wasn't the type of relationship that should be opened up to familial scrutiny, at least as far as she was concerned.

And she was still undecided during the next three days at work, which were hectic, leaving Regina neither the time nor energy to see Mateo in the evenings. One night, as soon as she got home, she got called back to the hospital again.

To make matters worse, she got a call from one of the administrators, who told her that Morgan Welk had filed a grievance against her, citing her "inability to allow specialists to do their jobs unhindered."

"It's not an official complaint," the administrator said cheerfully, as though it was no big deal. "Just an internal matter that will be dealt with on the administrative level."

"Send me a copy of the paperwork so I can file my answer," she said, keeping her cool, although the urge to curse was strong. "I'll only be here for another two weeks, so please do so immediately. I'd like to have the issue cleared up before I go."

"There's no need—"

"There's every need," she interrupted. "I will *not* have an unresolved complaint on my record."

Seeing the cardiologist later, she went out

of her way to treat him exactly the same way she always had, despite his smug, condescending manner. Obviously, he thought she should be cowering because of his grievance, but if so, she made it clear she was in no way concerned.

Although, of course, she was. Hers, to this point, was an exemplary record, and she'd be damned if the likes of Welk would spoil that.

The documentation came to her on Wednesday afternoon, and she read it through after she got home.

"He cited the Mignon case," she told Mateo when he came by that evening. She was striving for calm, but inside she was seething. Pacing back and forth in her minuscule living room helped, but only marginally. "Saying I gave the patient a doubtful prognosis while refusing to allow him to properly treat her TIAs or schedule her for heart valve surgery."

"But that case is still open," he pointed out. "We won't know for sure whether it's Fabry's or not until the genetic test results come back."

"Exactly." She jabbed a finger toward him in emphasis. "That's what Welk is counting on— that I'll be back in San Francisco by the time the results are in. And since I won't be here to make sure the complaint is expunged, it'll just remain on my record."

"An internal complaint like that won't hurt

you," Mateo said slowly, as though unsure of how she'd respond. "I mean, it's not a malpractice situation, or something the medical board would have to investigate."

She sighed, rolling her head, trying to ease the tension there.

"I know, but it still gets my goat that he'd do something so...so..."

"Underhanded? Ridiculous?"

"Either. Both. Ugh, that man just annoys me beyond reason."

Mateo watched her pace back and forth a couple times more, then said, "Hey, why don't you come to my place and stay the night. I have a heated pool, and we could swim, help you burn off some of that excess energy. I'll drop you off in the morning, when I'm going to work."

It was tempting. In all the time she'd been in Miami, and they'd been sleeping together, she hadn't been to his home, and he hadn't invited her again after she'd turned him down on the way back from the Keys.

She really was curious to see it, and would prefer to do so the first time without all of his siblings there.

"I'd like that," she admitted. "A lot."

"Go on, then," he said. "Grab an overnight bag, and let's go."

The house was very nice, but not as luxurious

as she half expected. And although it was silly, she was glad. While she'd gotten over her first hang-ups about Mateo being wealthy, it was nice to find his home to be comfortable and welcoming, rather than grand.

The lived-in atmosphere put her at ease as soon as they walked into the foyer.

"Make yourself at home," Mateo said as he guided her along a corridor toward the family room. Regina paused, looking at the photographs lining the hallway, trying to figure out who was who.

"Those are my parents," he said, pointing to a couple, arms around each other, laughing. "That was their twentieth wedding anniversary."

"You look a lot like your mom," she murmured, ridiculously moved to see his smile on his mother's face. "But it looks like you got your dad's eyes."

"Yeah," he said in that tender tone she'd come to recognize. "Cristóbal has Dad's smile, and Lola is just like Mom."

He pointed to pictures of his brother and then sister as he spoke.

"I can see that."

"And here's Ben, Micah and Serena," he said, indicating a more formal portrait, taken at a graduation. The younger of the men was of

Asian descent, while both the elder and Serena were African American.

"Ben's the oldest of the three?" she asked, trying to get them straight in her head.

"Yes, he's twenty-four now, and about to graduate from college with a bachelor-of-science degree. He's going to do his master's in chemical engineering. Micah is twenty-two, and he's very into music production, so he took a year off college and went to LA. It was with the agreement that if he wasn't making a living at the end of the year, he'd go back to school."

"How's he doing?" Regina already knew the answer to her question, just from Mateo's rueful tone, but she asked it anyway.

"Far better than I expected," he admitted. "I think I lost that round, but as long as he's doing well, I can't complain."

She laughed softly. "And what does Serena plan to study?"

"She's leaning toward medical research, which is why she picked University of Florida."

She contemplated the photographs once more. There was an older picture, which must have been taken not long before Mateo's parents died, since the entire family was together, and the three younger children were small. They were all smiling, Serena was in her father's arms, and the love between them all was palpable.

"Beautiful family," she said.

"My dad used to say we were a mini United Nations." Amusement and sadness were mixed together in his tone. "And after they were gone, I worried about being able to raise three kids of different racial backgrounds, and do it justice. Then I figured all I could do was raise them with love and honesty. I think they've turned out pretty well."

"I'm sure your parents would be proud—of them, and of you."

He'd thrown an arm around her shoulders as they talked, and he gave her a squeeze.

"Thanks."

As they continued down the hallway, she said, "I'm in awe of you, you know. I don't think I could do what you did."

"It's the kind of situation where you can't know what you'd do until you're in it," he said. "And it wasn't an easy choice to make." He hesitated for a moment, and then continued, "I'd planned to go into surgery. Renal transplant specialist was my goal. I had to modify that to make sure I was doing right by the kids."

"I'd wondered about that—what you'd given up to be there for them—and I'm sorry." She didn't know why, but the thought of his truncated dreams made her ineffably sad.

He stopped and pulled her around to face

him, and when he spoke, his voice was harsh and strong.

"There's nothing to be sorry about, Regina. I'm no martyr. In the final analysis, I didn't have to give up much of anything. My parents left trusts for all their kids, so I wasn't strapped for cash. I was able to get help from my aunt, and could afford a housekeeper, too. We had a roof over our heads, and food enough for any occasion. I don't need sympathy or accolades."

There was no way to explain that his fierce statement only made her prouder, and sadder, so she just smiled and said, "I don't care what you say. You're wonderful, and that's all there is to it."

"I'm not—"

But she didn't want to hear what he thought he was or wasn't. Not when she knew with all certainty exactly who and what he was.

So she pulled his head down and stopped him with a kiss.

When they came back up for air, she said, "So where's this pool? And more importantly, do I *have* to wear a swimsuit?"

"Do you honestly think I'm going to insist that you do?" he asked, nimble fingers already undoing her buttons, stripping her down.

And she laughed, desperately happy to move

past a conversation that made her feel so many emotions she didn't want to acknowledge.

She could handle Mateo in a carnal sense, but the tugs on her heartstrings were too much to deal with.

It had seemed so simple at the beginning. A chance to fulfil a fantasy.

Regina's reentry into his sphere had seemed prescient. Just as he was getting his own life back, she'd appeared, seeming to offer an adventure destined to get him out of his slump.

Well, she'd definitely brought all the excitement into his life that he could possibly need, but along with that, she'd brought a different kind of reawakening.

She made him feel alive, hungry for things he hadn't given much thought to.

Her passions reinvigorated his own; her ambition fired a corresponding desire to do well and do better than he had before.

Not that he wasn't proud of what he'd achieved. Yet, he knew he could go higher, do more.

He wanted more.

The problem was, part of that *more* he now wanted was her.

In his life, in his bed, forever.

And there was no way he could think of to approach a conversation about it that wouldn't have her running away.

She'd shared her parents' story with him, and he knew it had left an indelible mark on her. Even if she hadn't, Mateo had to admit to himself that one of her most attractive traits was her drive to be the best. The ambition that propelled her ever higher in her field.

There was no way he would ever stand in the way of her achieving her goals. Not when she'd worked so hard, and positioned herself so carefully.

Lying beside her in bed, her head on his chest and her even breathing soothing his soul, he dreamed, just for a minute or two, that he could follow her back to San Francisco. Woo her there and show her he was worth taking a chance on.

But that was just another fantasy.

When he'd taken up the mantle of raising his youngest siblings, he'd done so with the knowledge that it was, in a way, a forever job. Just because they'd gone to college, or in Micah's case moved across the country, didn't mean his part in their lives was over.

All of them, even he, needed the stability of their family home: a safe place, no matter what storms life threw at them. It had been over a decade, but they were nowhere near ready to give up what their parents had built and the security it afforded.

Even if all the others were ready to move on, Mateo knew Serena wasn't.

And his responsibility to her was solid and enduring.

It was too late to renege on the trust his family had put in him, and that was all there was to it.

It was hard to swallow, but he'd learned a long time ago some of the bitterest pills were and, in the end, they also were the best medicine. He wouldn't be the man he was today if he hadn't stepped up after his parents' deaths. Raising Ben, Micah and Serena had been tough, but in many ways he knew they'd done more to help him grow than he'd done for them. The trial and error of being a parent, the recognition that sometimes making a decision—even if it wasn't the best one—was better than not making one at all, had helped him become a better doctor.

As had the patience and ability to listen without judgment, which he'd had to learn.

No.

No matter his feelings for Regina, his family had to come first.

But the knowledge that she would soon be gone rattled around in his head, stealing his peace, keeping him awake. So he savored the warm weight of her on his chest, and committed it all to memory.

After all, in a short time, the memories would be all he had.

The next morning, when he was driving her home, he said, "Why don't you come by later for dinner? Lola, Micah and Cristóbal are flying in this afternoon."

But Regina shook her head, and it seemed to him they were once again on the same wavelength when she said, "No. Spend time with your family, Mateo. I'll meet them on Saturday night."

She was right, and her refusal was probably for the best, but it didn't stop it from hurting a lot more than he cared to admit.

CHAPTER THIRTEEN

It was ridiculous to be nervous about a party, but as Regina pulled up outside the Herrera house, her palms were damp, and she had to stop herself from obsessively checking her hair.

She, who would take on any doctor and stare them down until they cried uncle, was apprehensive about meeting Mateo's family.

Telling herself it didn't matter whether they liked her or not, since she wouldn't be around long enough for them to form a proper opinion, didn't make her feel any better. For all her cool containment—which seemed to have gone out the window anyway, where Mateo was concerned—she wanted to make a good impression.

She was only human, and realistically, nobody wanted to be disliked.

Giving her reflection one last, quick look in the mirror behind the sun visor, she forced herself to get out of the car and approach the house.

The front door was open, and when she stepped through, she found the foyer ablaze with lights. Balloons covered the ceiling, and their colorful, curled ribbons hanging down added a festive touch. Beyond the formal living room, the patio doors were open, and people spilled from the inside of the house to out by the pool deck.

As she stood there, gift bag in hand, Serena came in from the hallway leading to the kitchen and, seeing Regina, came to greet her.

"Hi," she said, smiling and holding out her hand. "I'm Serena."

"Regina," she replied, taking the outstretched hand to shake.

"Serena and Regina in the foyer."

The sing-song male voice came from behind her, so Regina looked over her shoulder to see Micah standing there. When she looked back at Serena, the young woman rolled her eyes.

"That's my brother Micah. Just ignore his attempts to turn everything into a rhyme. He can't seem to help himself."

"My rhymes mean money time," he said, giving them a grin. "Let me put that gift on the table for you."

When Regina held it out and thanked him, he took off with the bag, leaving her alone with Serena again.

Still nervous, Regina searched for something to say.

"Did you ever find your hoodie?"

Serena's brow wrinkled. "My hoodie?"

"Yes, you called to ask Mateo if you'd left it here..."

"Oh." Serena's confused expression melted away, to be replaced with a speculative one. "You were with Mateo when I called."

"Yes." *Way to keep a low profile, Regina!* "Did you find it?"

"Yeah, I did."

"Was it in the pile of clothes?"

Serena wrinkled her nose, and briefly pushed her lips to the side. "Yeah, it was."

Regina shook her head. "Don't you just hate it when they're right?"

That made the younger girl laugh, and agree. "Yes, I absolutely do." Looping her arm through Regina's, she started for the patio doors. "Come and join everyone outside. What can I get you to drink?"

Outside was bright with strings of lights, and gorgeous floral arrangements in pots were placed at intervals around the pool. The gazebo at the far end of the pool deck was beautifully decorated, too, with the bar and a table with snacks placed there.

The partygoers were clustered in small groups, and as Regina and Serena walked out, it felt as though every gaze turned their way. Serena towed her right over to where Mateo was standing, and his smile had warmth fanning out through her body, although she made certain to keep her smile neutral and polite.

Mateo greeted her with a chaste kiss on the cheek, which she returned.

"Glad you could make it," he said, and to her his voice sounded way too intimate.

"Sorry I'm late," she replied. She'd never let him know, but she'd dithered forever about what to wear, finally settling on a red sundress with a light cardigan.

"You're not," he replied, before turning to introduce her to the rest of his family.

She'd planned to stay in the background but found herself pulled right into the thick of things, not just by Mateo, but by his family, too.

It was evident how close they all were, as they teased and laughed, talking over each other in a way that made their bond easy to see. They'd sung a crazy rendition of "Happy Birthday," which seemed to be a family tradition, while Mateo hung his head as if in shame, although he was laughing. Regina should have felt left out, but instead, she couldn't help laughing, too, at their antics, enjoying the atmosphere.

And although she wandered away periodically to get a drink or some snacks, she kept finding herself gravitating back to Mateo's side.

Or he would come over to hers.

They orbited each other like planets destined to collide, and she didn't think their carefully casual attitude fooled any of his siblings.

They all sought her out at intervals, asking all kinds of questions, obviously trying to figure out exactly what kind of relationship she had with their brother.

She tried to make it clear that she was just in Miami for another couple of weeks, and then she'd be gone again, but that didn't really seem to satisfy them.

"I've been telling him it's time for him to get a life, now that the kids are out of the house," Lola said, giving Regina a straightforward look that put her on guard. "He's probably completely out of practice when it comes to dating."

Regina could tell the younger woman that her brother was in no way lacking in that department, but decided on a noncommittal sound instead.

"He's done so much to keep our family together, but he deserves the chance to get on with his life."

"I'm sure he does." She could picture it: Mateo dating, marrying a beautiful young woman, filling the house he grew up in with children of his own. She wished the future she imagined for him didn't make her feel so terribly sad. To mask it, she smiled at Lola and continued, "Give him time to sort himself out. He's been in one role for so long, it'll take a minute or two for him to decide what to do next."

Lola gave her a long, interrogatory look, then took a sip of her drink.

"I guess you're right. I just worry about him, alone here now. I want him to be happy."

Just then Mateo laughed at something Ben said, and Regina nodded toward him, unable to stop herself from smiling at the deep, happy sound.

"I think he is."

"For now," Lola said darkly, just as her girlfriend, Leticia, came over. When Lola smiled and put her arm around the other woman's shoulders, the resemblance to her brother made the breath hitch in Regina's chest. "Hey, babe. Having a good time?"

Regina was glad to be out of the crosshairs, but the melancholy sensation lingered long after the conversation had ended.

Lola was right. Mateo did deserve to go on with his life, and find happiness. He'd been an exceptional father figure to his youngest siblings, and would be a devoted and loving father to his own children when the time came.

And Regina was forced to admit to herself there was a part of her that wished she could be the one to provide that for him, but it would never be in the cards.

She'd never seriously given consideration to having children, too intent on making her way in the world, and excelling. Pushed by the need to prove herself and rise above the barriers others had tried to put in her way—from her father, to teachers and professors, and even some of her colleagues. There had always been someone telling her she wouldn't make it, and that had just made her work harder, fight more, for what she knew she deserved.

It was far too late now to have regrets for the path she'd taken. Too late to wonder what might have been.

This was reality, and Regina was a determined realist.

When she left to go back to San Francisco, she would leave with dignity, even while admitting to herself that Mateo meant more to her than she could ever have imagined possible.

Trust her to be ridiculous and fall in love at exactly the wrong time, and in exactly the wrong place, with exactly the wrong man. It just went to prove how right she was to have decided to put men—and all the problems they brought—behind her, but she wasn't sure Mateo would be that easy to get over.

If she could have fashioned a man specifically

for her, Mateo would have been the result: caring, responsible, loving and supportive. Even the fact that he was incredible in bed didn't rate as highly as those other attributes, although it was a definite plus.

But he wasn't for her, and she would never be able to give him all he deserved. Time to accept the fact, and put the best face on it that she could.

So, as she always did, she hid her thoughts behind a smile and reminded herself that this was a celebration.

And her heartache was nobody's business but her own.

It was great to have everyone back home for his birthday, but Mateo had to force himself to focus on his siblings rather than trail around after Regina like a puppy. Yet, no matter how he tried, he was always aware of where she was, who she was talking to, and what she was doing.

He hadn't even had a chance to tell her how beautiful she looked. The bright red of her dress set off her skin tone to perfection, and the slick of matching lipstick made him want to kiss her more than he wanted to breathe.

It had also been his plan to try to keep his siblings from asking her too many questions, but that hadn't worked out quite the way he'd wanted. He'd seen them all hovering around her at different times, no doubt cross-questioning her, trying to figure out what was going on between him and Regina.

Mateo wished he knew.

Oh, he knew what they'd agreed to, and what the plan still was.

They'd keep enjoying each other until it was time for her to go home, and then that was that.

But somehow, that didn't sit right with him now.

Didn't *feel* right.

Seeing her walk out of the house, arm in arm with a laughing Serena, had made his heart jump and kick into high gear.

And she'd fitted right in with the family, as though she'd always been a part of it.

As if she belonged there.

He was finding it harder and harder to contemplate her departure with any equanimity, but it had to be faced.

Regina had her life planned out, and it didn't include a man with a ready-made family tying him to Miami. A man who, in his midthirties, was just starting to get his life back together, and wasn't sure which way to go. And he would never contemplate burdening her with this change in his feelings.

He just loved her too much.

No one wanted Regina to succeed more than

he did, and he'd say and do nothing to stand in her way.

She walked over to the bar, and since she was the only one there, he finally saw a chance to talk to her by herself, where they weren't surrounded by nosy family members with big ears.

As he approached, she glanced up, and he saw a flash of something unreadable in her gaze, but she'd masked it behind a smile before he could figure out exactly what it was.

"Hey," he said, wishing he could put his arms around her, pull her close. "Are you having a good time?"

"I am," she said easily. "Your family is a lot of fun."

"That they are." He moved a little closer, and lowered his voice. "I'm always happy to have everyone home, but would it be terrible to say I wish they'd all leave, so I could have you to myself?"

She laughed lightly, but her lioness eyes darkened just a little.

"That's a horrible thing to say."

"I know." He tried to sound contrite but couldn't quite pull it off. "I'd ask you to stay, but I don't want to give them the wrong idea. I'd never hear the end of it when you leave. They all seem to like you a lot."

She hesitated, and he couldn't resist a spurt of

hope. Maybe she'd say she didn't care, and that she'd stay anyway, but that didn't happen.

"I like them all, too," she said and gave him one of those distancing smiles he hadn't seen from her in a long time, before glancing at her watch. "Enjoy your family, Mateo. I'm going to head home before it gets any later."

His heart dropped with disappointment, but he found the wherewithal to smile.

"Drive safely, and call me when you get home, just to let me know you made it okay."

The look she gave him made his heart turn over, and he suddenly didn't care who saw. He had to kiss her.

But he kept it gentle, although it wasn't the chaste touch of lips to cheek he'd given her when she arrived.

For a moment she melted against him, but then she stepped back, to give him a more genuine smile.

"None of that, now," she whispered. "The children will see."

And he laughed with her as they headed back over to the group and she said her good-nights.

He'd planned to walk her to her car alone, but Serena came with them, chattering away to Regina as though they were the best of friends, and the opportunity to give her a proper good-night eluded him.

He couldn't resent his youngest sister, though, and he slung his arm across her shoulders on the way back inside.

"So have you decided whether you want to transfer back down here or not?"

"No, I think I'll stay in Gainesville," she said, putting her arm around his waist and leaning her head against his shoulder. "It's not that bad, and the classes are interesting."

That pleased him, of course. Yet, he couldn't push aside the rush of loneliness her words brought, too.

But he would never let her know how conflicted he felt, so he squeezed her a little tighter and said, "Good girl. You worked so hard to get into that program it would be a shame to walk away from it."

She grinned up at him. "I know you just want me out of the house. So you don't have to pretend you're glad because I'm getting a college degree."

So challenged, he did what he'd always done when she'd teasingly sassed him in the past, and tickled her until she wrestled free and ran.

Later that evening, when all the guests were gone, and it was just the family, plus Lola's and Ben's girlfriends, the subject of Regina came up.

More like it was brought up and jumped on.

"So, what's really going on with you and the

Cali doctor, bro?" Micah tried to sound casual, but everyone else stopped talking to hear the reply.

Mateo shrugged, swirling the ice in his whiskey glass. "We're friends."

Clearly, that wasn't sufficient, since Lola got in on the conversation, too.

"I saw how you were looking at her. I think you're more than friends, and you don't want us to know."

"I like her." Serena was wrapped in a blanket on the couch. "She's cool, and easy to talk to. She was giving me some advice on which courses were best to take, and how to balance my time at school."

"She said she's going back to San Francisco in a couple of weeks." This from Ben, who had a speculative expression on his face. "Are you going to try one of those long-distance relationships? Those hardly ever work."

"And isn't she kind of...old for you?"

Micah sounded more intrigued than anything else, but Lola apparently thought his comment a step too far, and said, "Micah, *really*?"

"I mean…"

"That's enough." Lola called on every ounce of her second-oldest position to shut him down, and Mateo held up his hand.

"We're friends," he reiterated, keeping his

voice level, not letting his pain bleed through.
"That's all."

And although they all gave him a variety of
disbelieving looks, they got the hint and changed
the subject.

CHAPTER FOURTEEN

ON THE DAY after the party, Regina came to a decision.

She would enjoy the time she had with Mateo, without fear and without sadness.

Perhaps she should have been better prepared. She'd never been someone to do anything by halves, and having made up her mind to have a once-in-a-lifetime affair, might have expected to fall in love.

But she couldn't have predicted Mateo's effect on her life and her emotions. She'd felt immune from love, since the men she'd been involved with before hadn't really broken through the shell around her heart. No one had, until Mateo.

Knowing their relationship wasn't meant to last didn't diminish her feelings, or make her too afraid to carry it through to the end. They weren't hurting anyone—except her, and she was strong enough to bear it.

Yes, it would take her a long time to get over him, but surely she could do that, given the right mindset? Didn't she pride herself on her ability to focus on work, to the exclusion of all else? Right now, her focus was on Mateo: the way he made her feel, and her emotional connection to him, but she was sure her drive to succeed would return when she got back home.

Back to the place where the only thing of importance waiting for her was her job.

"No regrets," she reminded herself. "There's nothing to regret."

It had been a perfect interlude, with a man who set her afire in the best possible ways. Even the way he believed in her dreams made her more confident in herself.

He was the only person she'd ever felt secure enough with to show her fears, and be vulnerable with, and that was something she'd treasure, forever.

And seeing him with his family just reinforced her belief that he was where he was meant to be. They still needed him—Serena, in particular. When they'd talked, she'd seen the lack of confidence, the uncertainty in the younger woman's eyes, heard it in her voice. Mateo was his little sister's mooring in a world she'd learned could be unpredictable and filled with pain.

The bond Mateo and all his siblings shared went beyond the normal; it was forged in the loss of their parents and cemented by the care

Mateo had taken to keep his family together, whole and strong.

She envied them that sweet, solid connection. Having never known one like it, and having craved it as a child, she would never, ever do anything to damage or destroy it.

And that included telling Mateo how she felt.

He couldn't fool her; she knew she wasn't the only one battling with growing feelings and needs. That look in his eyes, the tender expression when their gazes met, told her far more than he probably wanted. It wasn't hard to distinguish between lust and caring, and Mateo cared for her, just as she did for him.

And that caring would keep them apart as firmly as if they hated each other, because trying to maintain their relationship would probably make both of them unhappy.

She couldn't bear the thought that eventually he'd regret not being with a younger woman, one who could give him a family of his own. And while they were definitely compatible now, how would their ten-year age difference play out in other ways, later on?

These were things she hadn't had to think about when she had so simply set out to enjoy his company for a while, but now they preyed on her mind.

No, it would be far better for her to go back to

focusing on her work and achieving her ambitions, and to keep this time with him as a sweet, lovely memory.

He called her on Sunday evening, after dropping Lola and Leticia at the airport. Serena had left earlier to make the more-than-five-hour drive back to college, and both Micah and Cristóbal had flown out earlier. Although Ben was staying another day, he had gone to visit friends in Vero Beach, and would be overnighting there.

"I'll come to your place," she suggested, when he asked if she wanted to get together. "You must be tired, and you're working tomorrow, aren't you?"

"Yes," he said. Even through the speaker in the car, his voice was a sexy rumble. "But I really want to see you. I'm already on the road, so why don't I just swing by?"

But she refused, and told him she would meet him at his house.

"We can go swimming again," she teased. The last time they'd set out to swim, they'd ended up making out in the pool instead.

He groaned. "Now you're just torturing me."

She laughed, already throwing some clothes into an overnight bag, even while still on the phone. "See you in a little while."

He greeted her as though he hadn't seen her in a month, rather than just a day, sweeping her into his arms and kissing her until her head felt light, and she was floating on a rush of desire.

Making love with him was never predictable, and when he lifted her and put her on the kitchen counter, she didn't know whether to protest or not.

Then she didn't have the mental capacity to do anything more than feel, and ride the waves of the orgasm he so easily created.

Mateo now knew his way around her body better than anyone she'd ever been with, almost as though he'd studied her and discovered exactly the places and actions that drove her wild. There was an added edge to him tonight, though, a fierceness that called to her own pain and determination to wring every last scintilla of pleasure out of their time together. It took their desire to a new level.

She stored up the memories. The way his hands felt, holding and caressing. His scent, so distinctive she'd know him in the largest of crowds. The sensation of his body under her, over her, in her.

The sweet way he whispered loving, joyous words into her ear, telling her how beautiful she was, how amazing she made him feel.

He made her feel beautiful, in a way she hadn't before. Not just physically beautiful, but from the inside out, and for that she'd always love him.

Lying next to him in bed later, she rested her cheek over his heart and listened to the strong, solid beat. How glad she was to have found him, to have loved him, even for this short time. While work had always been the center of her life, now she felt richer, more able to see past her own small box of a life.

She'd always considered love a weakness, something that reduced you to a diminished state, where you put others ahead of yourself, to your detriment.

Now she realized it was the opposite.

It made you want the loved one to have the very best in life, even if it meant letting them go.

The following morning, she got up at the same time as Mateo, and they had breakfast together. When they went outside to leave, his car wouldn't start.

"I'll drop you off at the hospital," Regina told him. "And if you want me to come back and be here when the tow truck comes, I can do that. I don't really have much planned."

"I'd appreciate it. But I don't want to waste your time doing all that. I can find out when Ben will be back, and get them to come for the car then."

"Don't be ridiculous. It'll be fine."

As she drew up outside the staff entrance at

the hospital to drop him off, he jokingly said, "I suppose kissing you goodbye is out of the question?"

She looked at him, noting that tender expression, as she shook her head. "Oh, no, you don't. You have your reputation to think about."

That made him laugh as he reached for the door handle. "Oh, being seen kissing you would definitely up my reputation around here, rather than diminish it."

Then he was gone, leaving her shaking her head, and chuckling, too.

That was another thing she liked about being around him. For so long, she'd taken herself and her life so seriously that she was rarely able to relax and cut loose. With Mateo she could do both.

It turned out there was nothing more seriously wrong with his car than a loose connection, and he called her around lunchtime to say the garage was sending someone to pick him up.

"I'll have my car back after work. The garage is not far from your place, so I thought I'd pick up some dinner and come by, if you're up for it?"

Of course, she said, "Yes. I'll see you then."

At a loose end, she called her friend Cher, who worked from home and often had time during the day for a chat.

"I haven't heard from you in ages. What's

going on? Still enjoying Miami? Although it must be almost time for you to head home."

"Less than two weeks left," she said.

Cher picked up on her tone, as only a good friend could.

"You okay? What's wrong?"

She didn't want to get into it; everything was too new and raw, but this was her oldest and most stalwart friend.

"Remember I told you about the man I went to that restaurant with?"

"Yes?"

"Well, I've been seeing him."

"Regina Montgomery, what are you telling me? Seeing him, like casually? Or seeing him? Like all of him?"

Despite all her pain, she had to laugh at her friend's way of expressing herself.

"Oh, I've seen every inch of him, and he is fine..."

The sound Cher made was somewhere between a whoop and a howl.

"Tell me everything, girlfriend."

It was a relief to let it all pour out, just set it all free, and ease some of the anxiety and hurt. Cher had always been a good listener and in Regina's corner, no matter what, and she was counting on her best friend to bolster her opinion of why a relationship with Mateo made no sense.

But Cher surprised her.

"I hear what you're saying, Reggie." Cher was the only person with permission to call her that, and she did it infrequently, usually when she was trying to make a difficult point. "But I also get the feeling that you haven't broached any of this with Mateo. How can you know if you're making the right decision without his input?"

"I don't think I could stand to get his opinion." She had to be honest, even though it sounded childish. "I know he cares for me, but…"

"But what?" Cher's voice was soft, but compelling. "You don't want to make the choice, do you? You'd rather be a martyr, letting him go so he can find this mythical younger woman and have babies, rather than ask him what he wants and risk it being you?"

"The fallout could be horrible." She was trying to be smart and reasonable, and it was beginning to annoy her that Cher couldn't see that. "I'm at least ten years older than him. If I'm lucky—and that's a big if—I'll hit menopause in about eight years, if not before, and he'll still be young and vibrant, while I turn into a hag. And what happens if, at some point along that continuum, he does decide he wants kids? How do I deal with that?"

Cher was silent for a few long moments, and then she said, "You know what I find interesting?" It was more of a preamble than a real question, so Regina didn't bother to reply. And as she expected, Cher continued, "You've hardly mentioned your career when talking about the situation."

"I did," Regina objected, thinking back on what she'd said. She had, hadn't she? "And you know that's of paramount importance, even if I haven't emphasized it."

"Hmm…" Cher had the knack of making the simplest sound seem like an interrogation. "Is it really the most important thing right now?"

"Of course." Yet, she almost didn't believe it herself, and her avowal was met with a sigh from her friend.

"I've never known you to be a coward, but you're acting like one now. Maybe you only think you're in love with him, but your feelings don't run as deep as you believe. If that's the case, you're right—it's better not to say anything to him until you figure out what's really important."

"Wow." A little stunned, and rather hurt, she said, "That was harsh."

"Not harsh, girlfriend." Cher said it softly, real sympathy in her voice. "Just truthful, as always. You're looking at his family and career, and your age and career, as impediments. You've made the decision for him about what's important, and what's not. I know you've never thought of love and relationships as vital, but maybe it's time you reevaluated all that."

"I honestly don't know what to do," Regina admitted. When was the last time she'd said that? She was so used to being in control of everything, having a set plan, that even to hear the words coming out of her mouth made her feel a little ill. "But I have a bit more time to decide."

"Put it out into the universe," Cher suggested, as she usually did whenever things were up in the air, or undecided. "And see what comes back to you."

Regina sighed. She really wasn't one for all those New Age types of things, but Cher was, and she'd never hurt her friend by telling her that reason and sober contemplation would trump whatever the ether had to offer.

"Okay, I will," she agreed.

"Let me know what you decide, Reggie. You know I'm here for you, whenever you need me."

They talked for a little more, and after they hung up Regina was as restless as she'd been before they'd talked. Maybe even more so, considering all the crazy thoughts Cher had put into her head.

Seeking something to take her mind off it all, she booted up her computer and started downloading the developmental courses she'd planned on doing while in Miami.

Before she got sidetracked by the sexiest man on the planet, and forgot about her plans and goals.

Funny how emotions messed with even the most level of heads.

Work had always been her solace, the one thing she could count on, without fail, to keep her going, so she went through the first course's lecture slides, and then took the first test.

But only half her mind was on it. The rest was watching the clock, thinking that Mateo should be leaving the hospital soon and coming to her.

It was aggravating and exciting, all at once.

As she rubbed the bridge of her nose, the thought came to her that if the universe had anything to say, it had better get a move on, because time was running out.

In twelve days, she'd be on a flight back to San Francisco, leaving all this behind.

The buzzer for downstairs went just as her email pinged. She got up to let Mateo in and unlock the front door before opening the message from her job in California.

Be careful what you wish for, she thought to herself, dazed and in disbelief after reading the email.

Mateo came through the door, took one look

at her face and said, "What's wrong? Are you okay?"

Through lips numb with shock, she said, "I just got offered the position as Deputy Chief of Medicine…"

And her heart ached with pride when he let out a shout, punching his fist into the air in celebration…

…even as that same heart broke, too.

CHAPTER FIFTEEN

WAS IT POSSIBLE to be proud and happy and miserable all at the same time, maybe with a side of angry thrown in?

Maybe not angry, Mateo reasoned to himself. More like resentful, and ashamed of himself for feeling that way.

He'd meant it when he'd snatched the obviously shocked Regina off her couch and swung her around, shouting, "You did it! I knew you would!"

Just as he'd meant it when he'd told her how pleased he was for her.

Yet, once the euphoria died down, reality had set in, and he'd recognized himself for a fool.

Somewhere in the deepest recesses of his heart, he'd hoped she wouldn't get just this kind of offer, because it gave her the ultimate reason to go back to San Francisco.

If they'd passed her over for promotion, maybe she'd get angry and decide to leave that hospital. Perhaps even move.

To Miami.

To him.

Of course, he'd been playing tricks with his own mind, even harboring such thoughts. Regina was well on her way to her goal, and even if the job offer hadn't materialized, she would have still been on track to make it happen.

Mateo knew he was just a diversion on her way to where she wanted to be.

But three days after hearing the news, while on his way to his Thursday clinic, he was still battling with his worst instincts, which told him to bare his heart and let her know how he really felt. That he was in love with her, and couldn't imagine his life, going forward, without her.

Nothing, and everything, had changed in the few short weeks since her reentry into his life.

His obligations to his family remained the same, as did her ambitions, but his love for her and the promise of her new job, which she'd worked so hard for, had turned everything on its head.

He'd had a brief moment of hope when she'd said, "I haven't replied. I need to find out what happened to Evan Logan, the doctor I thought would get the Deputy spot."

"Does it matter?" he'd asked, genuinely curious.

She'd nodded, her gaze unfocused and far

away. "Yes, it does. Was it that they wouldn't pay him what he wanted? If so, that's something worth considering. Worse, was he passed over completely? I'd still have to work with him, and if he's going to be resentful, I want to know that, too. If, on the other hand, it was simply that he didn't want the position, that's a different matter."

The way her mind worked truly amazed him. "How will you find out?"

That made her smile for the first time since he'd spun her around the room. "I have my ways," she said. Then she dropped her voice to an overly dramatic whisper. "There are spies everywhere."

There was nothing to do, he realized, but to accept that next week she'd be gone.

He should take a leaf out of her book and concentrate on work, to the exclusion of everything else.

He'd seen only three clinic patients, when one of the senior nurses came to find him.

"There's an urgent telephone call for you, Dr. Herrera. It's from the renal support network."

His heart skipped a beat, but he kept his cool. The support network, while it usually was the conduit through which they found organ donors for their patients, also provided other services. It wasn't unusual to field calls from them, but hearing the name never failed to give Mateo hope that one of his patients was about to be a lucky kidney recipient.

"Dr. Herrera," he said, picking up the call.

"Dr. Herrera, I'm calling to let you know we've found a match for one of your patients, Rexford Knowles."

For the second time in three days, he had the urge to punch the air in excitement, but this time he restrained himself.

"Is it a live donor?"

"No, Doctor."

"Local?"

"No, the kidney is being flown in from Texas. We have two possible recipients, but Mr. Knowles is first on the list. Please advise us as soon as possible if he's fit for surgery, and where the operation will take place."

The hospital didn't have a dedicated transplant team, so they either had to bring a surgeon in, or have the operation done elsewhere.

"I'll get right back to you on that. What's the ETA on the kidney?"

"The donor is on life support, and will remain so until early tomorrow morning, so you should have the organ by early afternoon tomorrow. I'll keep you updated."

"Thank you."

Then it was a flurry of activity.

Finding a surgeon was easier than he'd thought, since Tim Janowitz, who he'd been a resident with, had recently moved to Florida and was free the following day.

"I'd prefer to do the operation there," Tim said. "You'll be able to keep an eye on your patient afterward, rather than have someone he and his family aren't familiar with, post-op."

That was a relief, since Mateo had worried about the same thing.

Then, while one of the nurses made arrangements for the operating room and surgical staff, Mateo had to call Rex Knowles and his wife.

Pat Knowles tried to maintain her usual brisk, no-nonsense persona, but he could hear the fear and excitement in her voice as she said, "I'll get a bag packed and bring him around."

"I'll let them know downstair, to take him straight to a room, and I'll come by to examine him. Also Dr. Janowitz, the surgeon, will be by later to check his fitness to have the surgery."

He heard her deep breath and a whoosh of an exhale before she replied, "We'll be there in about an hour. Hopefully, the traffic isn't too bad."

And hopefully, Rex was well enough for the surgery.

And hopefully, the kidney was viable and got to them in perfect condition.

There were so many variables, but this might be Rex's last chance of survival. The decline in his health and his mental acuity had been marked over the last few months.

Turning to the nurse at the desk, Mateo said, "Could you contact whoever is on call today, and ask them to come in as soon as they can to take over the clinic for me? Also, advise Admissions that patient Rexford Knowles will be coming in for preoperative tests, and he'll be staying overnight."

"Of course, Doctor."

Once Rex got to the hospital, Mateo would be with him, doing full panels and screening, so as to have the results on hand when Tim Janowitz came in.

With patients waiting, he had to get his head back into clinic mode, but it was difficult. It was an unfortunate fact that they didn't have as many patients receiving kidneys as there were ones who desperately needed them, so transplants were dishearteningly rare.

He sent up a little prayer that all the variables came together, and then stepped into an empty office to call Regina and let her know what was happening.

When Mateo called her on the ward phone, rather than her personal one, she knew it was work-related, but that didn't stop her silly heart from turning over when she heard his voice.

Aware of being surrounded by people, including the odious Dr. Welk, who'd been called up for a consult, she made sure to keep her tone neutral.

"Yes, Dr. Herrera?"

"They've found a donor for Rex Knowles, and the kidney should be here tomorrow afternoon. He's coming in for pre-op testing, and I've already advised Admissions to send him right up."

All pretense of impartiality fled, and she said, "That's really great news."

"Let me know when he arrives, and I'm writing up the order for the tests I want run, so if you could get that started, I'd appreciate it. I only hope it works out well. So many things can go wrong."

The strain in his voice was real, and she wanted to reassure him, but from the corner of her eye, she could see Welk, not even pretending he wasn't eavesdropping. Yet, really, who gave a fig?

"We'll all have our fingers crossed for a favorable outcome."

When she hung up, she turned to find Welk standing there, a smarmy little smirk on his face.

"Taking personal phone calls on the hospital line is frowned upon here."

The drip of ice along her spine was a sur-

prise, but she pushed her instinctive defensiveness aside, so as to give him a narrow-eyed stare.

"Excuse me?"

He waved toward the phone. "You shouldn't tie
up the line with personal calls from men friends.
Those are for hospital business only."

The urge to smack his smug face was real
and visceral, but it wasn't the first time, and
it wouldn't be the last, she'd have to deal with
someone like him. So she hid her rage behind a
thin smile, before turning to the nurse who was
standing there, mouth agape.

"Ona, we're having a renal transplant patient
of Dr. Herrera's, Rexford Knowles, being admitted in a short time. When he gets here, please let
Dr. Herrera know, and get the panels started."

Then she turned to Morgan Welk, that dismissive smile still on her face. "Dr. Welk, I believe
there's a patient waiting for you in Room 436?"

She walked away then, before she could say
or do something that would make her lose her
cool completely.

He caught up to her, almost running alongside
her to keep up.

"I saw you the other morning, dropping Herrera off."

The way he said it, his tone, speared through
her. It made all the beauty of her experience in

Miami seem tawdry and wrong, and she felt her anger start to peak.

Stopping abruptly, she turned to face him, holding on to her temper by a thread.

"And?"

"And? You're a disgrace, running after that young man. You should be ashamed of yourself."

She loomed over him, glad of her superior height, and she knew her voice was shaking, but she didn't care. Her words were cold and precise. Measured.

"What is shameful is that you would spend more time speculating about things that are none of your business than you would looking after your patients. What's also shameful is that you bully and bluster your way around this hospital, rather than putting your mind to doing your job."

He sneered but stepped back, and before he could say anything, Regina continued.

"Luckily for me, I don't have to put up with you much longer, but I suggest you remember in the future that not everyone is frightened by your disgraceful attitude, and one day you may bite off more than you can chew."

Then she turned on her heel and walked away, and Welk had enough sense not to try to follow her again.

Ducking into a staff bathroom, she locked the

door and took several deep breaths, trying to dissipate the rage.

She wasn't ashamed, not in the slightest. It wasn't as though she was going to hang on to Mateo, or pretend she was right for him, but Welk's words clung to her like cobwebs, making her feel as though she needed a shower.

Was the entire hospital talking about it—about her and Mateo?

Like they had about her and Kevin?

Knowing Welk, he was probably spreading his poison far and wide, but it wouldn't hurt her, because she'd soon be gone.

Okay, that was a lie. It did hurt, and she had to admit it was because he'd brought up the age difference, and it, with all its implications, bothered her terribly. Not because there was anything wrong with a woman being ten years older than the man she dated. Hell, it could be a thirty-year gap, and still be all right. Men had been dating and marrying much younger women for centuries, and hardly anyone batted an eye.

And if Mateo had been married before and already had kids, she'd feel different.

But he hadn't. And he didn't.

So she couldn't be sanguine about any of it.

Mateo deserved the chance to be a father to his own children, not just his siblings.

Damn Morgan Welk and his nasty insinuations. He'd made her lose her temper, and it would probably earn her another one of his complaints.

They still hadn't got Kaitlyn Mignon's genetic test results back, and that was another annoyance to add on top of all the others.

Telling herself she had the offer of the Deputy Chief of Medicine job back in California should have made her feel better, but it had somehow refused to fully sink in. Intellectually, she knew it was hers for the taking, but whenever she thought about it, it didn't seem...real.

Maybe because she hadn't immediately jumped at the chance, the way she was sure she would have just five weeks ago. Instead, she'd been turning it all over in her mind, and had told the board she would speak with them when she returned home.

According to her sources, Evan Logan simply hadn't wanted the job. He was older, having gone to medical school after serving in the army, and had mentioned to more than one person that his main concerns at this stage were his grandchildren. If he took the job, he'd be spending even less time with his family, at a time when he wanted to spend more.

It was a sound decision, and cleared the way for Regina's advancement.

If she could just talk herself into being happy about it all, rather than wishy-washy.

Thinking about it allowed her temper to cool, and Regina shook her head. She washed her hands, her mind back under control.

This trip to Miami had stirred up nothing but trouble, and she should be glad it was almost over.

Of course, she was anything but.

Pulling open the bathroom door, she marched to Room 436, determined to hang over Welk's shoulder while he examined the patient.

She knew how much he hated that, and right now, she hated him just as much.

As petty as it may be, it was retribution time.

CHAPTER SIXTEEN

MATEO SPENT THE rest of the day assembling the transplant team, acting as transplant coordinator, supervising everything going on. He made sure all the instruments and equipment the surgeon would need were available. Then there were the surgical transplant nurses, dietician and social worker to be booked, provisional, of course, on whether the transplant actually took place.

There couldn't be anything overlooked or forgotten, not in such a specialized operation, and the aftercare of the patient was almost as important as the surgery itself. Rexford Knowles would have to learn a new way to live, to ensure the success of the transplant.

Luckily, Mateo had the ability and know-how to get things moving, but this was the first time he'd actually coordinated a transplant himself, so his tension built with each passing hour.

When Tim Janowitz arrived in the late afternoon, Mateo felt he had everything under control.

They shook hands, and the surgeon grinned at Mateo.

"Don't you age?" he asked in mock anger. "You look exactly the same as when I last saw you eight years ago, at that conference in Las Vegas."

Mateo laughed. "You don't look much different, either."

Tim pointed to his head and replied, "Except I don't have much left on top. How on earth can you still have all your hair?"

"Genetics."

"Yeah, that's the only thing that really works, isn't it?"

They went up to the surgical floor so Tim could approve the room they'd been assigned and look over the preparations Mateo had made. Then they went down to meet Rex and his wife.

When they got to the room, Regina was there, along with a nurse. Tim paused, then said, "I'm getting a flashback. It's like homecoming in here today."

"Good grief," Regina gave him a smile and held out her hand. "How are you, Dr. Janowitz? I haven't seen you since you finished your surgical residency at Charthouse."

"I'm well, thank you. I didn't realize you worked here."

Mateo shook his head, déjà vu rushing at him.

Regina and he had had a similar conversation when she'd just arrived, but suddenly it struck him, harder than ever, that she would soon be gone, forever.

The conversation swirled around him as Tim introduced himself to Rex and Pat Knowles, and then set about explaining the procedure for the following day. Regina slipped out of the room, after telling the patient she'd be back later.

"I'm sure Dr. Herrera has warned you that there's no guarantee that the kidney will be viable," Tim said, and Rex nodded. "Unfortunately, I can't make that determination until it gets here and I examine it, but I'm going to act as though the surgery is going forward, so as to make sure you're fully informed about what to expect."

Then he went through the procedure and the aftereffects. "You're going to be kept here in the hospital for a few days after surgery so we can keep an eye on you and make sure there are no complications. Until the new kidney starts producing urine, you might need to continue dialysis."

Pat Knowles looked concerned to hear that, but Mateo gave her a little smile, trying to be reassuring.

"Dr. Herrera has lined up all the specialists you'll need, including a couple of transplant nurses, who'll be here to look after you before you go home."

Mateo had gone through most of this with them before, but in his estimation, there was no harm in hearing it again. It was a major surgery, with potentially life-threatening effects. It was better for them to hear it twice and absorb it, than once and not remember.

On leaving the room, Tim said, "Regina Montgomery, eh? Remember how all us residents thought she was hot?" He glanced down the corridor, as though looking for her. "She's still damned gorgeous, isn't she?"

Mateo bit his tongue, not allowing the heated words building there to come out, knowing he was being ridiculous.

Tim sighed and grinned. "But now I'm a happily married man, with two-point-five kids. All I can do is look, nowadays."

"Two-point-five?" That was a safe subject. "Your wife is expecting?"

"Yep. Another little boy due in about four months. That'll make two boys and a girl."

"Congratulations."

"Thanks." They started walking to the elevator. "What about you? You have any kids yet?"

"No." He'd done his time, raising the youngsters, and didn't relish the thought of going through it all again. But he didn't elaborate.

While he'd known Tim for more than a decade, they weren't close friends.

Thankfully, Tim didn't pursue it, instead saying, "I want to tell you, I like the way you put this whole transplant together. I know this isn't something you do here very often."

Mateo shrugged. "It's a special interest of mine, and I knew this particular patient was high on the transplant list. I've been preparing for a while, networking to make sure I had the contacts, in case the surgeon wanted to do the operation here—like you did."

"It makes for a better recovery, in my experience, if the patient is familiar with his or her surroundings. He's comfortable with you as his nephrologist, and I trust you to keep an eye on him, once my stint with him is over."

"I've been treating him for about eighteen months, so, yes, we're pretty comfortable with each other, and maybe even more important, his wife is comfortable with me, too. She's the one who works hard to keep him on track."

Tim chuckled, "Well, everything looks to be in order, and the patient seems to be in good hands. Let's just hope the kidney is in acceptable condition when it arrives. Do you know the circumstances of the donor?"

"From the records that the support network sent over, it was an industrial accident that caused a traumatic brain injury. The donor is on life support until his parents arrive tomorrow morning."

The corners of Tim's mouth turned down, and he nodded soberly. "Well, thank goodness he'd signed up to be a donor. There are far too few people who do." His elevator came, and they shook hands before he stepped in. "I'll see you in the morning."

Mateo's phone chimed, and he took it out to see there was a message from Regina, saying she'd gone to get something to eat, but would be leaving to go home at about six.

Without a pause, he messaged back.

See you at seven.

If ever he was in need of her company, tonight was the night.

With the surgery set for the following day, he was on edge, but there was nothing else he could do to improve Rex's odds, so he'd rather spend the evening losing himself in Regina.

Regina walked through the door into her apartment and dropped her bag on the console table in the hallway, before going to the couch and flopping down on it.

What a day.

The residual effect of her run-in with Welk was still a bad taste in her mouth and had left her with the urge to punch something. Or someone. Preferably Welk himself.

Thank goodness she only had a short time more to deal with him.

Luckily, the rest of the afternoon had been mostly uneventful, and she'd had a chance to check in on Rexford Knowles before she left. He'd looked apprehensive, but still optimistic about the operation the following day.

"I know they said it wouldn't be a surety until they got the kidney here and took a look at it," he said. "But I'm staying positive and believing it's going to happen."

"Good for you." Regina discreetly checked his temperature and BP, and was relieved when they were both within normal parameters. The last thing they needed was for him to show signs of an infection. "Try to get some sleep tonight, although I know being here in the hospital makes that difficult."

"I'm used to it," he replied with a little shrug. His wife nodded, patting his hand.

"Well, hopefully, after tomorrow you can get unused to it again."

That made them both smile, as she intended. She really hoped the transplant would go ahead the following day, and be successful. Rex Knowles had been living on borrowed time.

And, she thought, how strange was it that the surgeon who would be operating was another of the Charthouse alumni? She'd seen the name on the chart but hadn't recognized it. Thinking back to how she'd easily remembered Mateo, after not seeing him for over ten years, she shook her head.

That alone should have been a red flag.

Glancing at her watch, she realized it was too late to think about showering before he got there. She'd left the hospital a little later than she'd planned, and he was invariably punctual.

Her mind circled back to Welk, and what he'd said.

Should she tell Mateo?

She chewed on her lip, considering it, then decided it wouldn't be a good idea. The two men already disliked each other, and this would just make Mateo despise the older man. When she was off in California and out of the situation, Mateo would be left to deal with the cardiologist here in Miami. There was no need to make a bad situation worse over her hurt feelings.

She'd just got up to get a drink of water when the buzzer went off, and she crossed instead to the door to let Mateo in. With just one glance, she could see the stress rolling off him in waves, and she walked right into his arms to hold him tight.

He buried his face in her hair and sighed.

"What a day."

"No doubt," she said, rubbing his back. "Have you eaten?"

"I had something at the hospital, late in the afternoon. I'm not hungry."

"I know what you need," she said. The idea had popped into her head, and seemed a great one. "A bubble bath."

He leaned back to look at her, eyebrows up in his hairline.

"A what?"

She grinned at his bewildered expression. "A bubble bath. Nice and hot."

He wrinkled his nose. "But won't I smell like a flower garden?"

"You can shower after, with some manly soap, and we'll never speak of the flowery scent again."

That had him chuckling as she led him through to the bathroom and set the bath. One thing she'd enjoyed immensely about the apartment was the deep, long bathtub, and they put it to good use.

They started out facing each other, legs entwined, and Mateo talked about the preparations for the surgery the following day, as though obsessively trying to make sure he hadn't forgotten anything.

To divert him, she said, "How crazy is it that another of my Charthouse residents is doing the operation? You're all coming out of the woodwork."

He smiled, resting his head back against the wall, his eyes half-closed. "I was surprised when I saw his name on the surgeons' list. The last I heard he was in Illinois."

"Do you know what brought him here?"

"No clue. Maybe he got tired of the winters, although I think he was originally from Maine or some other northern state." He sat up a little straighter and said, "You know what I don't like about this bubble bath?"

"What?"

"The bubbles." He waved his hand through the froth. "They hide your body."

She laughed and carefully shifted around, so as not to cause a tsunami onto the bathroom floor. Settling back against his chest, with his legs on either side of her hips, she asked, "Is this better?"

"Mmm-hmm," came his reply, as he stroked along her arms. "Much better. Your skin is so soft I can't stop touching you."

There was a note in his voice that made her glad she couldn't see his expression, which she knew would be tender. Loving.

Having her back to him made it easy to joke.

"Yours will be, too, with all the flowery moisturizer in the bubbles."

He chuckled, as she meant him to, but his hands shifted to her breasts, and suddenly she wasn't laughing anymore.

No fear. No regrets.

Those words drifted through her mind as she sank into the delicious sensations Mateo created with those talented hands and fingers.

But soon they were in danger of trying something silly, like making love in the slippery bathtub, so they quickly showered off the bubbles and retired to the bed.

There was an urgency to the way Mateo touched her, and she forced him to slow down, wanting to savor each moment, each kiss, every caress. She wanted the chance to love him, so he'd always remember her and the nights they'd shared.

It was made more magical by the bitter knowledge that there would only be a few more nights like this, and she stretched out their pleasure, taking control in a way she rarely did.

And when he groaned her name, it was one of the sweetest sounds she'd ever heard.

Afterward, she curled up against his side, in the position she'd learned was her favorite. When they slept together, they'd end up spooning, but before they fell asleep, she lay listening to his heartbeat, content and replete.

"There's something I want to tell you."

His voice was soft, and something about the timbre of it made her pulse go haywire. It was on the tip of her tongue to tell him she didn't want to know—that whatever it was, was best left unsaid—but before either of them could say anything more, his phone rang.

Mateo cursed, and she rolled out of his way, relief at the interruption making her feel a little weak as she turned on the bedside lamp.

"Yes, Mateo Herrera here."

His face tightened as he listened to whatever was being said on the other end of the line, and fear suddenly gripped her.

Was there something wrong with Rex Knowles? With the donor?

Or was it something to do with one of his siblings?

"Yes, I'll be there as soon as possible. Let me know when you get in touch with Dr. Janowitz."

He was out of bed, heading for the bathroom, as he said over his shoulder, "The donor's family got there early and said their goodbyes. The kidney should be here in about four hours."

As she heard the shower start up, Regina sat on the edge of her bed, clutching the sheet in both hands. She didn't know where the fear had come from, when he'd said he had something to tell her, but it had rendered her ice-cold, terror-struck.

And she knew why.

She didn't want him to tell her how he felt. What would happen if she were too weak to re-sist admitting how much she loved him, too?

Call it cowardly, but she couldn't face that. Not now, with all her resolutions to walk away made shaky by the force and beauty of his lovemaking.

"Saved by the transplant," she whispered to herself, knowing she had time to get herself to-gether before such a moment may arise again.

Hoping she had the strength to stick to her plan to leave, and not falter.

CHAPTER SEVENTEEN

THE TEXT CAME at two in the morning, and Regina was half-asleep, having tossed and turned, unable to fully surrender consciousness, worried about what was going on.

"Thank goodness," she muttered, reading the message that the kidney was viable and the surgery was underway.

Get some sleep.

His order made her shake her head, both because he knew her so well, and because he wouldn't follow his own advice. No doubt he'd stay at the hospital until he knew the outcome of the operation, even though he wasn't actually in the OR.

But somehow, probably from a mixture of relief and exhaustion, Regina actually did fall asleep, so deeply that when her alarm went off, it was startling.

She rushed through her morning routine, getting to work early and going straight to the surgical ICU unit to check in on Rex Knowles. Tim Janowitz was there, examining the still-sedated patient, and she waited outside the room for him to finish and come out.

"Morning," he said, looking surprisingly chipper for a man who'd been up most of the night. "The patient's doing really well. I think we'll have him out of bed for a little while later."

"Good to hear," Regina replied, knowing that it boded well that Tim wanted Rex ambulatory so soon. Although that wasn't unusual, if there were any complications during the surgery, getting patients out of bed would be postponed. "I take it everything went well?"

"Very well. The kidney was in really good condition, and there were no surprises during the operation itself. Now we just have to wait and see how it functions, and hope his body doesn't reject it."

He started walking toward the doctors' lounge on the ICU floor, and Regina walked with him. It was on the tip of her tongue to ask where Mateo was, but she restrained herself.

"Pat Knowles has gone home?" she asked instead.

"Yes. I sent her home, telling her we were going to keep her husband under for a while, and she should get some rest." At the door of the lounge, he added, "Do you have a few minutes? I want to ask you something."

"Sure. I came in a little early, so I have time." He held open the door for her, and she stepped through, saying, "What can I do for you?"

The lounge was empty, and Tim made a beeline for the coffee machine. "Coffee?"

"No, I'm good." She held up her travel mug. "I have some."

Once Tim had his filled cup, he waved her to a seat and sat at the table across from her. He looked serious, and Regina's curiosity was piqued.

"So, what's up?"

"I wanted to ask you about Mateo."

Her heart skipped a beat and her stomach dropped, but she kept her expression as neutral as she could, even as her brain whirred. Was Tim asking in a professional capacity, or a personal one? Had Welk's nasty comments and speculation reached even a surgeon who didn't work at the hospital but had been brought in for one operation?

There was only one way to find out.

"What about him?"

"This is confidential, okay?" Tim waited until she nodded, before continuing. "I moved down here because I was offered a job at a new hospital being built north of Miami. It's still under construction, but they offered me a salary, office space and the ability to pretty much freelance until they're ready for me, because otherwise I'd have extended my contract in Illinois, and not moved."

"Okay," she said, her pulse kicking into high gear. Was this the same hospital Mateo had mentioned? The one in Plantation? Something stopped her from asking. It was better if Tim was allowed to tell the story in his own way, but she wished he would get to the point.

"One of my jobs is to assemble my own team, for when the hospital opens, and I think Mateo would be a great candidate."

Yes!

Regina took a sip of her coffee to hide the elation she was sure had sparked in her eyes. This was what Mateo had hoped for but hadn't been sure was achievable, and she was so proud and happy for him that she felt fit to burst.

"I want your opinion of him, since you've been working with him, and I trust your judgment."

The elation drained away, leaving her feeling cold and trapped.

"Are you asking for an official recommendation?" she asked carefully. "Because there are a couple of issues I have with giving one." When his eyebrows rose, she lifted a hand and added quickly, "Not reservations about Mateo's capability, but realistically, I've only worked with him for the last five weeks. That's not a long enough time to fully assess someone professionally, especially when they're in a different department."

Tim nodded. "Understood, and no, I don't need anything in writing, just your observations."

"One last thing," she said, determined to be completely honest. "Mateo is…my friend. So I may be a little biased."

To her surprise, Tim just shrugged.

"Doctors recommend their friends for positions all the time, so I don't see the big deal."

He obviously hadn't picked up on her hesitation, and had taken "friend" at face value. She probably shouldn't be surprised at that, or hurt, but she was.

It seemed just one more indication of how mismatched they were, if people were either disgusted or disbelieving that they could be in a relationship.

Yet, she had to put that all aside, if it would help Mateo.

Assuming her business persona, the one that had seen her through all of the hardest parts of her life, she said, "From my observations he's a dedicated nephrologist, willing to work with other doctors to get to the root of a patient's disease. He's not territorial, but will fight for his patients, and isn't intimidated when people try to bulldoze him. I think his bedside manner is exemplary, too, and his patients seem to trust him."

Tim nodded, holding her gaze. "He put together that transplant like a pro, and I know it's not something he does every day. I've had less well-organized surgeries at established transplant hospitals."

She didn't have a useful response for that, so she just nodded, taking another sip of her coffee.

But the wheels were turning in her head, and her brain ping-ponged between excitement at the opportunity seeming on offer for Mateo, and dread if their affair became public and it came out she'd vouched for him.

"When will you speak to him about this?" she finally asked. It would give her a better idea of how to handle the information.

"Sooner, rather than later." Tim rolled his shoulders, the events of the night probably catching up with him. "The hospital will be operational in about six months, and I need to get my staff in place. I'll also need to figure out if he has a contract in place here, and whether he can get out of it." He sighed. "I can't wait to relinquish the hiring responsibility to the administration, when we're up and running. I don't like this part of the job, at all. I'd rather be in the OR, hands-on, helping people."

She smiled and pushed back from the table, ready to take her leave.

"Well, good luck with your new endeavor," she said, shaking the hand he offered. "And remember my caveats when giving you my answers to your question."

Tim smiled and walked her to the door. "I remember you from back in my Charthouse days. You were tough but fair, always scrupulous in how you handled things. You word carries some weight with me."

Regina nodded, giving him as much of a smile as she could manage.

Scrupulous? She didn't feel that way, at all. In fact, despite her joy for Mateo, she felt completely unscrupulous.

Not that she hadn't told the truth about his abilities, from her perspective, but she was in love with him, so how unbiased was she, really?

As they exited the doctors' lounge, she saw Morgan Welk further along the corridor, and the way his eyes narrowed. He started toward them as she took her leave of Tim but walked right past her, without even acknowledging her presence.

"Dr. Janowitz," she heard him call. "A moment, please."

What did Welk want with Tim?

Regina had to stop herself from looking back, not wanting to seem concerned, even as her heart rate went up a notch and her stomach clenched.

She'd taken the coward's way out by not being

completely truthful to Tim, and now there was the added worry about what Welk was up to.

She had to figure out how to handle the situation.

If she somehow messed up this opportunity for Mateo, she'd never forgive herself. He'd been so supportive of her goals and ambitions. If she owed him anything, it was reciprocity in that respect.

What would be best?

Going back and telling Tim the truth of their relationship?

Maybe reiterating that her recommendation was strictly unofficial?

Something else completely?

This new wrinkle in their relationship threw her into crisis mode.

She couldn't be sure what Mateo had been about to say the night before, but if he had been about to make some kind of romantic declaration, she was even more glad he'd been forestalled.

There were more important things than their feelings at stake. His family. His future.

Regina wouldn't let anything destroy or damage what he'd built.

She was still desperately running through her options when she got to the fourth floor, and had to force herself to fully concentrate on getting ready for rounds.

Losing herself in work usually centered her

thoughts, but it took all her energy to keep her focus. On a break, she saw there was a text from Mateo, saying he'd gone home for a nap but was now back in the hospital, and asking what she wanted to do that night.

It was Friday night, which meant he didn't have to work the following day, while she was still on call.

She already knew what she had to do when she replied to his text, telling him she'd come by his place later, after she got everything squared away at work.

Putting her phone back into her pocket, she realized her hands were shaking, and she left the cafeteria to go to the ladies' room and try to pull herself together.

She'd hoped to keep seeing him until she left, but it was getting too hard to manage her emotions. Now it was easy to put aside all other feelings and concentrate on the fact that his dream of working for a dedicated transplant unit was within his reach.

She'd make sure nothing stood in his way.

Especially not her.

Mateo yawned, almost nodding off in his chair as he waited for Regina to arrive. The short nap he'd had earlier hadn't really revived him, just given him enough energy to get through the rest of his shift and make it home.

He was grateful that Regina was coming to him this evening, rather than the other way around. She'd messaged to say she'd be a little late, but that was okay. He didn't mind waiting.

Regina was worth waiting for.

And tonight he'd tell her how he felt, and ask her to keep seeing him, even after her time in Miami was over.

He'd thought it through. At least he'd tried to. But he'd be the first to admit his emotions, his love for her, tended to muddle his thinking. Yet, he was sure they could work something out. It wasn't optimal, but maybe they could do the long-distance thing for a couple of years, until Serena got fully on her feet.

Then he'd be willing to move wherever she wanted, just so they could be together.

It was funny that he would feel that way, considering it meant, once more, giving up what he wanted for the sake of love. Yet, he didn't resent the thought. His parents' lives and deaths had taught him the most important things in life weren't actually things, but people.

Regina was as important to him as any of his siblings, even though he knew he couldn't let go of the family reins just yet.

That sense of having been entrusted with his

parents' wishes hadn't diminished. Not even after eleven years. That responsibility had to be fully taken care of before he could move on, and he thought Regina would understand that and, hopefully, be patient.

What they had was too special to throw away.

But when he opened the door to her, he found her almost unrecognizable, and the sense of being thrown back in time by her distancing smile kept him silent, stilling the urge to take her in his arms.

And if nothing else, this Regina Montgomery was completely efficient.

As efficient at breaking his heart as she had been putting her patients at ease, or Morgan Welk in his place.

She turned and looked at him, her lioness eyes clouded, but direct.

"I've decided it's best that we don't see each other socially, for the rest of my time here."

Each word was a blow, but he wanted to understand, so he could, just as efficiently, plead his case.

"Why?"

It looked as though she were about to shrug, and he was glad when she didn't. Any sign of nonchalance would have set him off.

"It's time to put this behind us and start looking ahead," she said cryptically. "I have a lot to do, professionally, before I go back, and I don't need the distraction."

Was that what he'd been? A distraction? Nothing more?

He wanted to ask her, but his pride wouldn't let the question pass his throat.

Hell, he could hardly breathe, much less articulate.

She shifted, one hand coming up slightly from where it hung at her side, and then falling back.

"I've had a great time with you. You know that. And I hope you had fun, too. But I have to start concentrating on my future, and these last few days that I'm here are valuable. I don't want to waste them."

So he'd been both a distraction and, apparently, a waste of her time.

He felt the first spark of anger but tamped it down. If he allowed his rage to overcome him, he didn't know what he might say.

"Okay." His voice was rough, rusty, passing with painful difficulty through his tight throat. "If that's what you want."

For a moment, a brief hopeful moment, he thought she might change her mind. It was there in her eyes, in the glimpse he got behind the mask she'd donned to speak to him.

Then it was gone, and she nodded.

"It is."

At least it seemed she knew better than to thank him, or try to initiate some tender parting moment. Instead, she just walked away and let herself out, leaving him there, feeling as though he'd been hit by a truck.

How long he stood there, staring at the door, he didn't know. The sound of her vehicle had faded, and the murmur of the television was the backdrop to his numbness.

Not even the anger, which had so briefly stirred inside, came back to sustain him.

He was…empty.

Shell-shocked and dead inside, because the only woman who'd ever touched his heart and soul had just tossed him away like he was a used tissue she no longer needed.

And he didn't even have the wherewithal to wonder exactly why.

CHAPTER EIGHTEEN

YOU CAN DO THIS, REGINA. Make it through the next seven days, before you go home.

But she wasn't absolutely sure she could.

She hurt, even physically, whenever she thought about Mateo. She hoped he was all right. That the shock and hurt she'd seen in his eyes on Friday night had morphed to anger or indifference. Either of those would be preferable to seeing him in pain.

Or having him look at her with contempt.

She had enough of that for herself, without him horning in on the act.

Thinking she'd be safe from seeing him over the weekend, she remembered too late that he'd undoubtedly be in to check on Rex Knowles, and she went to ICU on Saturday morning.

When she got there, Rex was sitting up. The improvement in his appearance was marked, and wonderful to see.

"It's working already," he told her with a wide grin. "The kidney is actually working, so they've taken me off dialysis. Dr. Janowitz is transferring me out of ICU today, although he wants me to stay in the hospital another night or two."

"That's wonderful," she told him, even though her stomach twisted. If he was transferred back down to the fourth floor, there would be no avoiding Mateo. All she could do was hope Rex would be sent to one of the other floors instead.

That was when it dawned on her that, as his nephrologist, of course Mateo would want to check on his progress personally, and before she got a chance to scuttle back to the fourth floor, Mateo walked in.

Her heart turned over, and it took every ounce of strength to greet him with cool professionalism.

He replied in kind, his expression frozen, his gaze blank. Then they both looked away, and Regina said goodbye to Rex before beating a hasty retreat. She'd held it all together this far, but she wasn't sure how strong her composure actually would be under prolonged exposure to the man she loved.

And she definitely wasn't strong enough to survive an interrogation, should he put her to one. Hell, just a simple question might break her.

Which was why she'd avoided calling Cher, the one person she could count on to tell it like it was. Her friend had already pointed out facts

Regina didn't want to think about right now. Instead, she preferred to concentrate on the good she was doing for Mateo, rather than anything else.

Nothing could convince her that she hadn't done the right thing. He'd been through too much, given up too much, to have anything more taken away from him. Mateo deserved the world on a string, and everything in it as his own.

He deserved a woman who could give him everything he could ever need, or want, and that was not her.

And if she kept reminding herself of that fact, she might feel a bit better.

Hopefully, Rex would be sent to one of the other floors, but she wasn't so lucky, and later that afternoon, he was indeed transferred back under her care.

There was no way to avoid seeing Mateo again, later that afternoon.

"Regina."

Oh, the ice in Mateo's voice, as he nodded his head in her direction. Unlike earlier, now his gaze was angry. When it snagged hers, her blood froze, but Regina refused to let the pain show.

"Mateo. Here to check on Rex Knowles?"

"Yes. He's doing exceptionally well."

"So I see from his charts."

"I'll leave instructions for his care, for overnight, but I'll be back periodically over the weekend to keep an eye on him."

That sounded almost like a threat, despite his banal, curt tone, and it was more agonizing than she'd expected, and that was saying a lot.

She'd been expecting to hurt, but not this much. Surely it would be less painful to have him just plunge a knife straight into her chest.

"Excuse me," she murmured, affixing a habitual smile to her lips. "I have a patient I have to deal with."

And she forced her trembling legs to propel her away before she lost all control and started to cry.

She avoided him as best she could over the rest of the weekend, feeling like the coward Cher had accused her of being, and the strain of it had her dragging by Monday morning.

Not even seeing Kaitlyn Mignon's genetic test results, and finding out the Fabry disease diagnosis was correct, lifted Regina's spirits, although she was glad for the younger woman's sake.

"Please forward these results to the patient's primary care physician," she instructed the nurse at the desk, remembering to smile, although for the last few days her face had felt stiff. As though it didn't actually belong to her.

Glad of something to distract her, she made the decision to call Kaitlyn herself and alleviate some of the stress the other woman clearly exhibited regarding her ailments. Waiting for the report to get to her physician, and then hoping they'd quickly pass on the news, seemed cruel when she could just handle it herself.

And she was glad she had, when Kaitlyn, clearly in tears, wouldn't stop thanking her.

"I know you said there's no cure, and maybe I don't qualify for the treatment, but just knowing, after all this time, is such a relief. I don't know how to thank you for that, Dr. Montgomery."

"Just take care of yourself," she said, not wanting or needing the thanks. "And there are both support groups and organizations with information that will be helpful to you. The best thing to do will be to learn as much as you can about the disease, and then you can advocate for yourself, or at least know who to turn to, so they can help if you hit a roadblock."

After hanging up, she took another look at the report, and realized she didn't even care enough to forward it to the administrator who'd handled Welk's complaint. That could die a natural death, as far as she was concerned. It meant less than nothing.

All she wanted to do was make it through today and the two days after that without losing her mind, and then she could go home and lick her wounds in private.

Then the administrator called and asked if she could stay another day, as the doctor she was acting for couldn't come in until Friday.

"Her baby is ill, and her husband couldn't get Thursday off to take care of him."

Regina's flight wasn't until Friday, and although she really wanted to say no, it would have been churlish, so she agreed.

Now, if she could just minimize her contact with Mateo, she'd be okay.

Right?

Mateo tried to remind himself that no one had died. That the end of his relationship with Regina was no comparison to when his father's Cessna had gone down in the Everglades, and he, along with his siblings, had been orphaned.

But the sensations he was experiencing seemed to belie that assertion.

The cycles of numbness, anger and bone-deep pain were familiar, even after all these years. The force of will it took to keep going, and put one foot in front of the other, was the same.

Each time he saw her, the anguish was amplified, until he could hardly stand it. When he heard through the grapevine that she'd been asked to stay on another day, he was torn between anger and gratitude. His head wanted her gone—sooner rather than later—but even now his heart wanted her to stay. Forever.

Because it was clear, even in the midst of his pain, that his feelings toward Regina hadn't changed, and if nothing else, he deserved to understand why she'd rejected him the way she had.

Surely the connection he felt when they were together wasn't completely one-sided?

Even if she reiterated her disinterest in continuing their love affair, she owed him more of an explanation than she'd given.

He knew he had to talk to her, but he wasn't ready. His emotions were too raw, his anger too sharp. Trying to have the conversation he knew they had to have would have to wait until he achieved some modicum of control.

Maybe, he thought in the middle of Tuesday night, when he was trying to work it all out, she needed an opportunity to work through her own feelings. Perhaps, although it would hurt more than he wanted to contemplate, he should let her go back to San Francisco. Give her some time back on her home turf before following her, and making a declaration she couldn't ignore.

So on Wednesday he put in for a week off the following month, and booked a ticket to San Francisco.

Rex Knowles was one of the few bright spots in the days following Regina's bombshell. The transplant recipient was so happy to be alive and feeling better that no amount of warnings about the antirejection drugs and what he needed to do to stay healthy would bring him down.

"Dr. Janowitz is supposed to come to give me one last checkup," he said on Wednesday afternoon. "And then it's up to you to send me home."

"What, are you tired of us already?" Mateo couldn't help teasing, happy to see the other man smiling, the unnatural pallor he'd developed over the course of his disease starting to dissipate.

"Well, of you, sure." Rex's grin was cheeky. "But I really don't mind that Dr. Montgomery. She's easy on the eyes."

Keeping the smile on his face after hearing her name was almost impossible, but somehow, he managed it.

"I said the same thing." Tim's voice, coming from behind him, startled Mateo, and he turned to see the surgeon already at the foot of the bed. "Much better-looking than this mug."

Mateo didn't answer, and was thankful when the conversation moved to the surgical site and postoperative care.

Tim and he left the room at the same time, and although he didn't feel like having a conversation, Mateo forced himself to walk with the other man.

"I actually need to talk to you. Do you have some time?"

"Sure."

"Walk with me down to my car."

Under different circumstances, Mateo would be intrigued, but nothing mattered right now, except perhaps politeness.

Tim didn't start talking until they were outside the hospital and heading toward the car park.

"I want to know if you'd be interested in coming to work with me, at the new transplant hospital in Plantation."

They were passing a bench, and Tim sat down, then looked up at Mateo expectantly.

It was what he'd wanted, the next best dream to his original one of doing the surgery himself, but he felt no enthusiasm. No spurt of adrenaline brought on by surprise and delight.

Yet, that was no reason to dismiss it out of hand.

Just like the pain of his parents' passing had eventually faded to bearable, if he couldn't win Regina back, her loss would, too.

"I would be," he said, sitting beside Tim. "Tell me more."

As Tim outlined what he was involved in, and the role he envisioned Mateo taking, a small spark of interest was kindled deep inside. By the time Tim finished, and they had talked about his status at his present job, and whether he would be able to leave it without difficulty, Mateo realized the fog he'd been battling was lifting.

Just slightly, but enough to give him back some hope for the future.

"I'm actually very surprised Regina didn't mention it to you," Tim said, capturing Mateo's complete attention. "Even though I asked her not to, I didn't think she'd keep that promise."

"You spoke to her about this?"

"I asked her opinion of you, as a doctor, and if she thought you'd be a good fit for what I was looking for. She gave you a solid recommendation, but she did warn me that you were her friend. I got the impression she was telling me she wasn't unbiased, without coming right out and saying it."

"We were more than friends." The words popped out of his mouth, propelled out by a brain churning to work all this new information out, mold it into something that made sense.

"Duh," Tim said, sounding like he was doing an impression of a twelve-year-old girl. "Wait, were?"

"Yeah, she broke it off, last Friday."

"Huh. That was the day I spoke to her." Tim got up and stretched. "And in case you were wondering, even knowing the two of you were an item, I still trusted Regina to be honest with me.

I saw your capability for myself, too, but I still valued her opinion. She was always a straight shooter. I'll be in touch."

Mateo stayed where he was after Tim walked away, turning all he'd heard over in his head, trying to fit the pieces together.

He'd been about to tell her he loved her, ask her to wait for him. He'd been willing to give up his life in Florida for her.

Had she realized that?

And knowing he was about to achieve his dream of being on a dedicated transplant team, decided that was more important than their relationship?

Or did she really not feel anything for him, the way she'd implied?

There was really only one way to find out, and one person who could tell him the truth.

And he was no longer willing to wait to find out what that was.

CHAPTER NINETEEN

REGINA HAD DAWDLED at the hospital for so long that by the time she'd decided she needed to go home and get some sleep, it was almost eight o'clock, and exhaustion tugged at her every muscle.

Thankfully, she hadn't seen Mateo that afternoon, although she wasn't actually sure whether she was thankful or not. She'd seemed to spend an awful amount of time looking for a glimpse of him, as though compelled by forces beyond her control.

It was long past the time he normally left the hospital, barring emergencies, so as she dragged herself down to her car, the last person she expected to see was him.

He was leaning on the wall in front of her vehicle, and her first muddled thought was to wonder how he'd known where she'd parked. After all, there were three staff parking levels.

There was an urge to turn and walk away, but she wasn't one to run, so she kept going toward him, even though she got the sense that she was walking into some indefinable danger.

"I need to talk to you." His voice was hard, but she couldn't tell whether with anger or hurt. "We can do it here, but it might get loud, and I don't know if you want an audience like that."

She narrowed her eyes, unsure of whether he really meant that, but she wasn't willing to take the chance. Not with him behaving so uncharacteristically.

"I'd prefer not to air my dirty laundry in public," she told him, tipping up her chin to let him know she was in no way intimidated. "But I'm still on shift, and I need some rest. Can't this wait?"

"Your place or mine, then," he said, as though he hadn't heard her question. "Your choice."

She sighed, trying to appear nonchalant, when her pulse was all over the place. "Just come to my place. It's closer."

"I'll drive." It wasn't a request, or a question, and when he waved her toward where his car sat, three spaces away from hers, she decided discretion was the better part of valor, and preceded him there.

The short trip to the apartment was undertaken in silence, and Regina didn't try to break it. She was using the time to muster her defenses, staring out the window so she wouldn't stare at him instead, but just being in such close proximity was delicious torture.

Still silent, they went into the building. There was a group of young people in the lobby, already waiting for the elevator, and they all got in together.

One of the young women eyed Mateo in the mirrored door and flipped her hair, as though trying to entice him into talking. Regina didn't know how he didn't notice, but when she shifted her gaze to Mateo, it was to find his fixed not on the other woman, but on her.

It was impossible to look away. His eyes were fierce and wild, and the heat that rolled through her abdomen and flared out into her veins was a visceral reminder of the passion between them.

The got out on her floor, and she fumbled with her keys, her trembling fingers refusing to cooperate. Mateo took them from her, and the brush of his fingers sent a jolt of electricity up her arm.

Once inside, she dropped her bag on the console table and turned on the lights.

"I spoke to Tim Janowitz this afternoon."

She wanted to face him, to pretend this meeting meant nothing to her, but she couldn't. So she walked over to the sliding glass door overlooking the city lights, and watched his reflection instead.

"About?"

"About a job on a dedicated transplant team. He said you knew about it."

"He asked me not to say anything, so I didn't."

Mateo paced closer, and she saw him stab his fingers through his hair, as though in frustration.

"Did that have some bearing on you breaking up with me?"

She wasn't a good liar. Had never cultivated the art, since she despised people who glibly told untruths without batting an eye.

"Some," she admitted, leaving it there.

"Did you do it because you knew I loved you, and would have passed up the opportunity to be with you, if you asked me to?"

She closed her eyes for an instant, wishing they didn't have to do this, or that it didn't tear her up to have to tell him the truth. But they had gotten to this point, and maybe only the truth, all of it, would do.

"Tell me, Regina. If you don't love me, don't want me, then just tell me."

His hand tore through his hair again, and her heart broke at the angry, pain-filled gesture. Finding courage from somewhere deep within, she turned and faced him, finally.

"This…thing between us was beautiful and glorious, but it's not meant to last. I can't be all that you need or deserve."

His eyes narrowed, and he stepped closer.

"What kind of answer is that, Regina? It was a simple damn request. Tell me you don't love me, and don't want me, and this conversation will be over, and you can fly back to California to the job you've always wanted."

She almost laughed then, at him thinking she was throwing him over for a job, but her chest was too tight with agony to spare the breath.

"I'm too old for you." It came out as a whisper, each word cutting her throat at it passed. "You deserve someone who can make a home for you, give you kids, not a driven loner who's never been able to sustain a relationship, not even with her own family."

"No. No, no, no, Regina. You don't get to come into my life, make me love you, make me need you almost as much as I need air, and tell me BS like that. I don't need to hear whatever cockamamie excuses you've come up with in your head to make this seem right."

He was so close now she could feel the heat pouring off him, and it took everything she had not to reach for him, to seek the solace she so desperately wanted in his arms.

"Tell me you don't love me."

"I broke up with you because I knew we couldn't last—"

"Tell me you don't love me."

"And I didn't want Tim to use my recommendation and then find out we were sleeping together—"

"He's not a fool. He knew we were sleeping together. Tell me—"

"And I didn't want to disappoint you, later on—"

"Do you think I care about any of this—about a job, or your age, mythical kids I don't even want or anything else—more than I love you?" His voice was low, vibrating with so much anger he might as well have shouted.

"Your family needs you, and you need them."

He shook his head. "Nothing can come between me and my family, but that has nothing to do with you and me, and whether you love me."

He reached out, as if he couldn't help himself, and traced his finger down her cheek. Then he drew his hand back, and the fierce light in his eyes almost took her to her knees.

"You know what to do to get rid of me, Regina. Just say four little words: I don't love you."

"I can't."

The admission was dragged from her throat, and had hardly emerged before she was locked in his embrace, and he was kissing her, as though never to stop.

When his lips left hers, it was to trace a path to her ear, and he whispered, "Nothing else matters, Regina. Believe me. Only love. Everything else is just window dressing."

"I'm afraid." If there was going to be truth, then it needed to be complete, so he could understand. "Afraid that I won't be enough for you. That I won't know how to balance a life with you, and still be true to myself. And afraid I'll hurt you, or your family, because I don't really know how to be a part of a unit as close as yours."

He leaned away so he could see her face.

"Do you love me?"

There was no avoiding it and, truth be told, she didn't want to avoid it anymore.

"I love you so much it hurts."

His eyes gleamed, and he had that tender set to his mouth that had first told her how he felt about her.

"Then we'll make it work, however we have to. Didn't you tell me, a while back, that there's nothing you set your mind to that you can't achieve."

"That's true."

"Then just set your mind to loving me, and we'll take care of the details later."

"I can definitely do that," she said, cupping his face. And setting her mouth against his, she whispered, "Easily."

EPILOGUE

"ARE YOU SURE?" Mateo sounded stunned.

He leaned across the table, as though getting closer and searching her expression would give him some information he was missing.

Regina smiled and reached for his hand. Twining her fingers around his, she gave them a squeeze.

"Perfectly," she replied, her smile widening as she watched him try to process what she'd just said.

Outside the restaurant's windows, lights gleamed on the dark waters of San Francisco Bay, and the trees undulated in the cool, salty breeze. They were at a secluded table for two, at her favorite high-end eatery. Mateo had flown in the day before, and she'd hugged her news to herself, wanting the setting to be perfect before she revealed it.

Although, with the way they'd made love, ravenous for each other after almost a month apart, nowhere could be as perfect as being in his arms, hearing him declare, over and over, his love for her.

"Which hospital?" He didn't so much ask as fire the question at her—a true sign of his discombobulation.

Only once had he ever been that forceful when talking to her, and it was the night he'd gotten her to admit to loving him.

When she answered his question, his eyes widened.

"That's a premier hospital. One of the best in the state, if not *the* best."

She chuckled. "You sound surprised. Didn't think they'd want me?"

"Darling, any hospital that gets you is lucky," he replied, still sounding a little dazed. "But it's a step back, isn't it? I don't want that for you."

How could she have ever thought that a job, of any kind, could be more important than the love of a man as true, noble and supportive as Mateo?

"It really isn't," she reassured him. "Think of it this way—in the normal course of things, the position they've offered me is exactly what I was expecting to get here, and—" she held up her hand to stop him from butting in "—*and*, it's at a more prestigious facility. I'll be second in line for Chief of Medicine, and they already know that's what I'm interested in, in the long run."

He chewed on the side of his lip, looking so adorable doing so she wished she could kiss that spot, soothe the sting of his teeth. Then, as he pulled back his hand and she noticed the distant, faraway expression in his eyes, a little trickle of cold water ran down her spine.

Mateo had told her that once Serena was out of school, he'd be willing to move to be with her, and the enormity of his proposed sacrifice had driven straight through her heart.

Give up his home in Florida, and with it his post as linchpin for his family? And also give up, after only a few years, his dream job?

For her?

It didn't seem right, even as she recognized it as proof positive of his love.

"We can travel back and forth," he'd said. "As often as we can. Or meet somewhere in the middle, if that works better. I could buy a place in Texas, so we'd always have somewhere to go that's halfway for each of us."

When she'd thought about it, that didn't sit right with her.

Oh, she had no doubt they'd both make the effort, but with his new position and its attendant unpredictability, and the duties she'd take up as Deputy Chief, they probably wouldn't see that much of each other.

And she'd learned, perhaps far later in life than most, how important it was to be happy personally, as well as fulfilled professionally. There was no way she was waiting four years to be with Mateo on a permanent basis.

Regina had never been a halfway kind of woman. She was all or nothing.

Now, watching him wrestle with what she was saying, she wondered if she'd somehow got it all wrong. If he didn't see this as the perfect solution.

She was willing to make the sacrifice instead, and take a job in Miami to be with him, but his reaction made her doubt herself, and him.

"I thought you'd be happy," she said slowly. "That you'd see it as a good thing."

His gaze snapped to hers, and before she realized what he was going to do, he was on his feet, and tugging her up, too, into his arms.

It was only then that she realized he was trembling; his hard, warm body was shaking with some undefinable emotion. And his eyes were anguished as he gazed deep into hers.

"Darling," his voice was hoarse, choked, little more than a whisper. "My darling love. I would love nothing more than to wake up every morning for the rest of my life, and see you beside me. To go to bed and know you're there. Reach for you. Make love to you. But I never, ever, want to hold you back. It would kill me if you ever looked at me with disdain and accused me of getting in the way of your dreams."

Her heart soared then, as she lifted her hand to press the palm to his cheek.

"Mateo, I love you more than I ever thought I could love, and there's nothing that's going to keep me from your side. Not my job, or yours. Not even your family. This is my new dream. To be yours, and have you as mine, forever. Is this a dream we can share, and be happy with?"

He kissed her, uncaring of the appreciative audience around them, and she grew hot, melting into his body, as he ravished her mouth.

"You have just made me the happiest man in the world," he said. "And there's nothing more that I could ask for."

"She said yes," the woman at a nearby table stage-whispered to her companion. "Isn't it romantic?"

Regina felt an unaccustomed wave of heat rising into her face, and turned toward the window, so no one would see her blush. Somehow that comment made her self-conscious and unsure.

Mateo dipped his mouth close to her ear and whispered, "I change my mind. There is one more thing that I would ask for. Will you marry me, Regina? I have this ridiculous urge to tie you to me in every possible way known to man, so you don't stride off into the sunset without me."

A bubble of laughter rose into her throat, but it got caught on the wave of love swelling in her chest.

"I will. I'm yours, my love," she replied. Then a mischievous urge arose in her as she thought back to when they first met. "And I will be, for every shift hereafter."

* * * * *

*If you enjoyed this story, check out
these other great reads from
Ann McIntosh*

Christmas with Her Lost-and-Found Lover
Best Friend to Doctor Right
Awakened by Her Brooding Brazilian
The Nurse's Christmas Temptation

All available now!